Courtney Crumrin

By Ted Naifeh

Crumrin

The Coven of Mystics

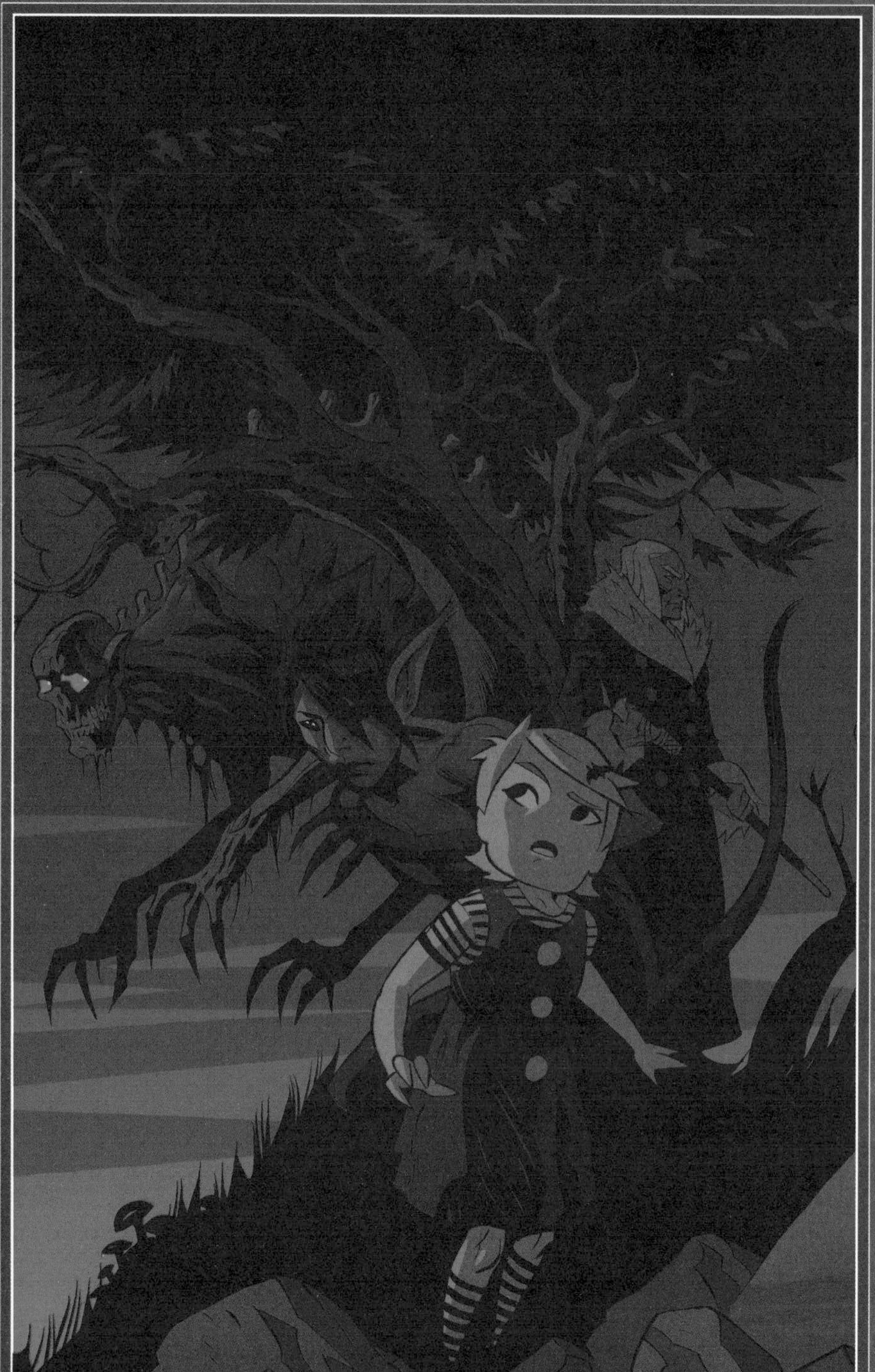

Courtney Crumrin

By Ted Naifeh

The Coven of Mystics

Written & Illustrated by

—◈— TED NAIFEH —◈—

Colored by

WARREN WUCINICH

Original Series edited by
JAMES LUCAS JONES

Collection edited by
JILL BEATON

Design by
KEITH WOOD AND ANGIE DOBSON

Oni Press, Inc.

founder & chief financial officer, JOE NOZEMACK

publisher, JAMES LUCAS JONES

v.p. of creative & business development, CHARLIE CHU

director of operations, BRAD ROOKS

marketing manager, RACHEL REED

publicity manager, MELISSA MESZAROS MACFADYEN

director of design & production, TROY LOOK

graphic designer, HILARY THOMPSON

junior graphic designer, KATE Z. STONE

digital prepress lead, ANGIE KNOWLES

executive editor, ARI YARWOOD

senior editor, ROBIN HERRERA

associate editor, DESIREE WILSON

administrative assistant, ALISSA SALLAH

logistics associate, JUNG LEE

Originally published as issues 1-4 of the Oni Press comic series
Courtney Crumrin and the Coven of Mystics.

1319 SE Martin Luther King Jr. Blvd.
Suite 240
Portland, OR 97214

onipress.com · tednaifeh.com

First Edition: January 2018

ISBN 978-1-62010-463-7
eISBN 978-1-62010-024-0

1 3 5 7 9 10 8 6 4 2

Library of Congress Control Number: 2011933144

Printed in China.

For Kelly

'ILLSBOROUGH'S A SAFE PLACE TO RAISE YER *KIDDIES*, SO LONG AS THEY *KNOW* TO STAY OUT O' THE *WOODS*.

NASTY THINGS LURKIN' ABOUT.

LIKE *ME*, FER INSTANCE!

SQUEEE!

MOST O' THE LITTLE TYKES LEARN TO KEEP *AWAY*.

BUT YOUNG *COURTNEY CRUMRIN*, SHE'S A DIFFERENT *STORY*.

WILLFUL LASS.

SHE THINKS SHE'S GOT THE *BETTER* O' OL' BUTTERWORM.

SUPPOSE SHE'S *RIGHT*, TOO.

A GIRL WITH 'ER POWERS GOT *NOTHIN'* TO FEAR FROM AN OL' BUG-A-BOO LIKE ME.

COURSE, THERE'S ALWAYS A *BIGGER* BUG-A-BOO.

7

Chapter One

HEAR ME, DARK AND DREADFUL ONES, HORRENDOUS CHILDREN 'NEATH COLD STONE.

RELEASE THY MOST ACCURSED SON, TO SERVE MY NEED AND MINE ALONE.

AWAKEN, FIEND FROM DEPTHS UNKNOWN, I BID THEE, RISE FROM SUNLESS LANDS,

TO RENDER FLESH FROM BLOODY BONE,

TO FEAST ON GORE AT MY COMMAND.

HEH HEH.

YEH SHOULD'VE BEEN FASTER, BROTHER.

⟩ULP⟨

OH BUGGER!

"MISS CRUMRIN?"

I'M *SORRY* TO *BORE* YOU, MISS CRUMRIN.

BUT *SURELY* AMERICAN HISTORY ISN'T *THAT* DULL.

MUST BE THE WAY YOU *TEACH* IT THEN...

WHAT WAS THAT?

SORRY, STAYED UP *LATE.* HOMEWORK.

I SEE.

UNDER THE *CIRCUMSTANCES* I CAN ONLY BE *SO* SYMPATHETIC.

CRUMRIN

WHAT'S *THIS!?!*

A *ZERO.*

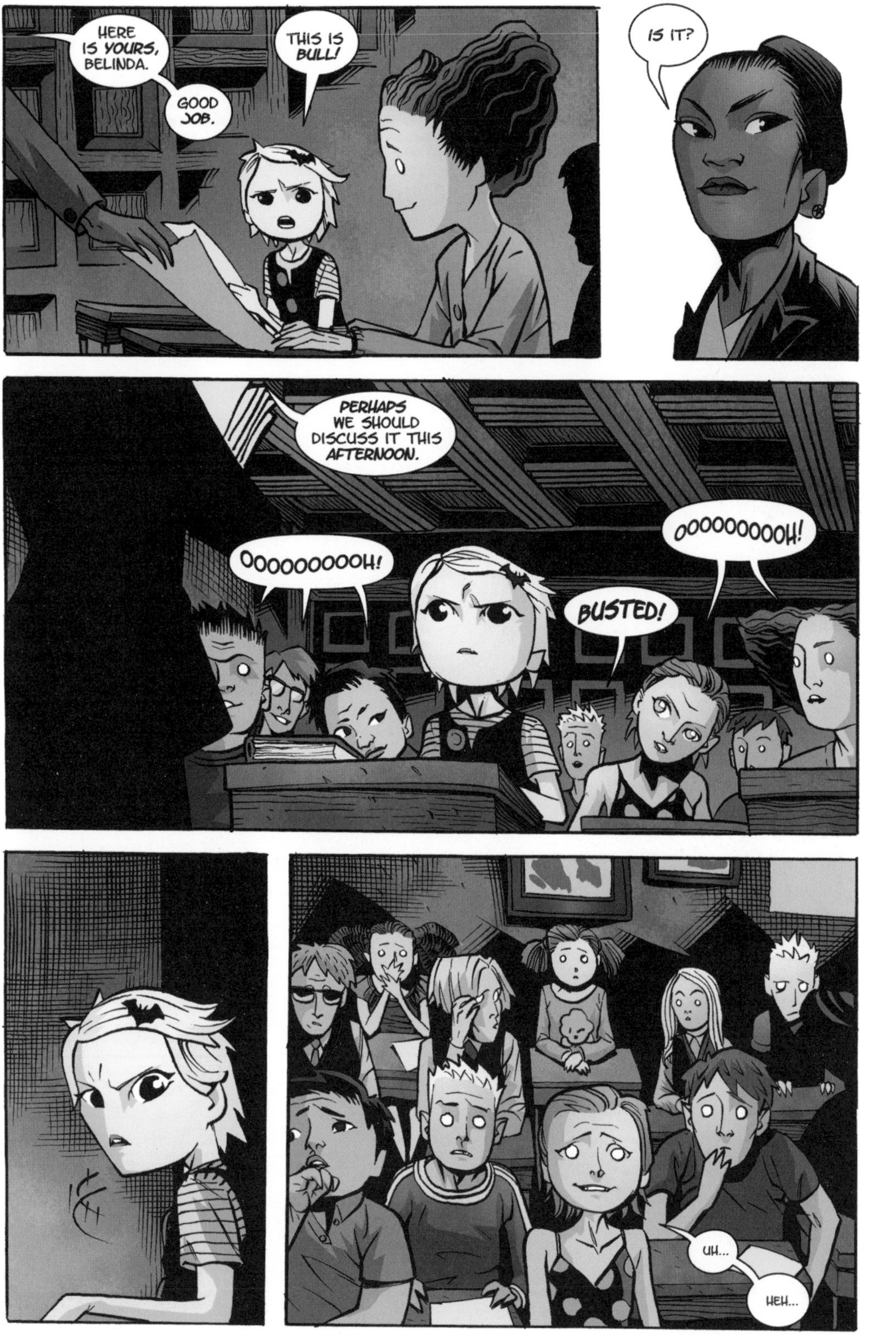
HERE IS YOURS, BELINDA.
GOOD JOB.
THIS IS BULL!
IS IT?
PERHAPS WE SHOULD DISCUSS IT THIS AFTERNOON.
OOOOOOOOOH!
BUSTED!
OOOOOOOOOH!
UH...
HEH...

IT WAS NOW TWO WEEKS INTO THE NEW SCHOOL YEAR, AND COURTNEY WAS BEGINNING TO NOTICE THAT HER NEW TEACHER, MISS CRISP, WAS A DREADFUL NUISANCE.

THERE WAS NOTHING WRONG WITH THE HOMEWORK, OF COURSE. THE COMPLEX COCKTAIL OF ENCHANTMENTS HAD REQUIRED WEEKS OF RESEARCH, BUT NOW A BEWITCHED BELINDA BLOOM HANDED IN TWO COPIES OF HOMEWORK EVERY DAY, ONE WITH COURTNEY'S NAME ON IT.

THE ENSORCELLED GIRL NEVER EVEN REALIZED SHE WAS DOING IT. AND COURTNEY WAS NOW FREE TO DEVOTE HER FULL ATTENTION TO HER GROWING OBSESSION, HER UNCLE'S LIBRARY OF WITCHCRAFT.

SHE HAD NO INTENTION OF ALLOWING THIS MEDDLESOME WOMAN TO RUIN THINGS.

I HAPPEN TO *KNOW* THAT PAPER WAS PERFECT.

I HAD MY *PARENTS* DOUBLE-*CHECK* IT.

OF *COURSE* IT WAS PERFECT. BELINDA'S HOMEWORK IS *ALWAYS* EXEMPLARY.

THE *IDEA* IS FOR YOU TO DO IT *YOURSELF*, AND ACTUALLY *LEARN* SOMETHING.

YOU THINK *BELINDA* DID MY HOMEWORK FOR ME? SHE DOESN'T EVEN *LIKE* ME.

YOU HAVE TO HAVE *FRIENDS* TO CHEAT THAT WAY.

OR *OTHER* POWERS OF PERSUASION.

I... DON'T KNOW WHAT YOU'RE *TALKING* ABOUT.

YOU THINK I'M *BLACKMAILING*—

COURTNEY, I HAPPEN TO *KNOW* YOU'RE GETTING AN *EXCELLENT* EDUCATION FROM YOUR *UNCLE.*

HOWEVER, THERE ARE CERTAIN THINGS YOU'RE *NOT* GOING TO LEARN FROM *HIM,* AND YOU'LL *NEED* THEM TO LIVE IN THE *ORDINARY* WORLD.

DO YOU UNDERSTAND?

...

YES, MS. CRISP.

SCREW THE ORDINARY WORLD.

OVER THE LAST YEAR, COURTNEY CRUMRIN HAD SETTLED COMFORTABLY INTO HILLSBOROUGH. SHE FOUND THAT, GENERALLY, THE ENVIRONMENT WAS TO HER LIKING.

SHE'D MADE FEW FRIENDS AMONG THE LOCAL CHILDREN, AND THAT ALSO WAS TO HER LIKING, FOR THEY WERE NOT.

BUT THE STRANGE OLD NEIGHBORHOOD WAS AT LAST BEGINNING TO FEEL LIKE HOME.

THE FOREST STIRRED SUDDENLY, AND COURTNEY FELT AN AWFUL THRILL TICKLE HER SPINE.

SOMETHING WAS COMING.

SOMETHING... UNSPEAKABLE.

WHATEVER IT WAS SOON PASSED BY, BUT COURTNEY HUDDLED IN THE UNDERGROWTH FOR AN HOUR AND SHIVERED UNCONTROLLABLY.

NOW HER ONLY THOUGHT WAS TO REACH HER UNCLE.

A RICH HELPING OF DREAD AND HORROR HAD BEEN STUFFED DOWN HER THROAT.

HER INSIDES WERE STILL WRITHING FROM THE EXPERIENCE, AND SHE BARELY NOTICED THE STRANGE MEN ON THE DOORSTEP.

EXCUSE ME, MISS.

WE'RE LOOKING FOR PROFESSOR CRUMRIN.

UNCLE A, I NEED TO **TALK** TO YOU.

COME IN, MY DEAR.

GENTLEMEN.

COURTNEY, WOULD YOU WAIT IN THE SUNROOM WHILE I DEAL WITH MY GUESTS?

SURE.

UNCLE ALOYSIUS RARELY HAD VISITORS, AND NEVER ENCOURAGED THEM TO LINGER.

COURTNEY KNEW THERE MUST BE OTHER WARLOCKS, BUT UP TILL NOW, SHE HADN'T MET ANY.

SHE WASN'T SURE SHE LIKED THE LOOK OF THEM.

I UNDERSTAND YOUR RELUCTANCE, BUT FRANKLY, MY DEAR FELLOW, THERE'S NO ONE ELSE WITH YOUR EXPERTISE.

WHAT ABOUT MADAM HARKEN?

SHE KNOWS AS MUCH OF THESE MATTERS AS I. PERHAPS MORE.

PERHAPS.

BUT THE COMMITTEE HAS FAR MORE CONFIDENCE IN YOU.

I'M HONORED.

EXCELLENT. SO IT'S SETTLED.

YOU DON'T SEEM TO *APPRECIATE* THE *GRAVITY* OF THIS MATTER, ALOYSIUS.

PROFESSOR, WHAT ABOUT THE *MANDRAKES*? *JACK* AND THE *CHILDREN*?

INDEED. THANK YOU FOR *THINKING* OF ME.

I HOPE YOUR *NEXT* CHOICE PROVES MORE *FRUITFUL*.

JACK *MANDRAKE*, THE SELF-PROCLAIMED *GREATEST* WARLOCK OF THE AGE?

SURELY HE ISN'T IN ANY *DANGER*.

HAVE YOU NOT *HEARD*?

PROFESSOR, THEY'RE *DEAD*.

LAST *NIGHT*.

THE CHILDREN AS WELL?

HECTOR HERE IS DOING HIS *BEST*, BUT HE *JUST* ISN'T EQUIPPED TO DEAL WITH... *YOU KNOW*...

NIGHT THINGS.

NOT LIKE *THIS* ONE.

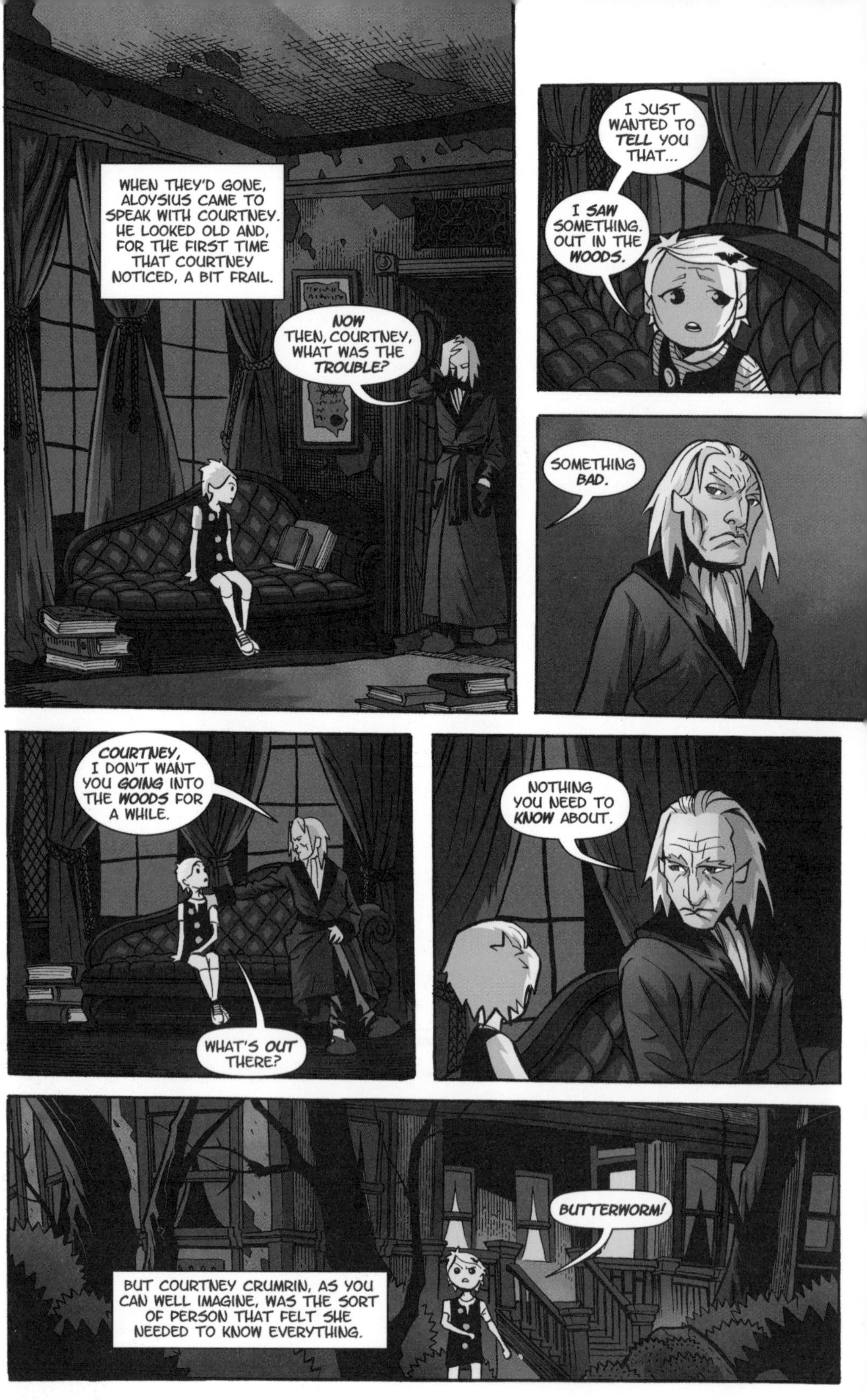
WHEN THEY'D GONE, ALOYSIUS CAME TO SPEAK WITH COURTNEY. HE LOOKED OLD AND, FOR THE FIRST TIME THAT COURTNEY NOTICED, A BIT FRAIL.
NOW THEN, COURTNEY, WHAT WAS THE TROUBLE?
I JUST WANTED TO TELL YOU THAT...
I SAW SOMETHING. OUT IN THE WOODS.
SOMETHING BAD.
COURTNEY, I DON'T WANT YOU GOING INTO THE WOODS FOR A WHILE.
WHAT'S OUT THERE?
NOTHING YOU NEED TO KNOW ABOUT.
BUT COURTNEY CRUMRIN, AS YOU CAN WELL IMAGINE, WAS THE SORT OF PERSON THAT FELT SHE NEEDED TO KNOW EVERYTHING.
BUTTERWORM!

C'MON, BUTTERWORM.

DON'T MAKE ME GET MY DAD'S ELECTRIC CLIPPERS.

WHAT YEH WANT?

AND KEEP YER VOICE DOWN, GIRL, FER GOODNESS SAKE.

WHAT IS IT, BUTTERWORM? WHAT'S OUT THERE?

OH, 'IM? THAT'S OL' TOMMY RAWHEAD.

BEEN AWHILE SINCE HE COME OUT O' THE MARL-PIT.

TOMMY RAWHEAD?

WHO IS HE?

COURTNEY WISHED FOR SOME DAYS AFTERWARD SHE HADN'T ASKED. IT SEEMED THERE WERE SOME THINGS SHE DIDN'T NEED TO KNOW AFTER ALL.

THE GOBLIN SMILED ITS NASTY LITTLE SMILE.

AND THEN IT TOLD COURTNEY ABOUT THE WORST HOBGOBLIN THAT EVER WAS.

"WE *GOBLINS* BEEN AROUND A *LONG TIME.* SOME ARE BAD, LIKE *ME.* SOME ARE *WORSE.*

"OL' TOMMY, HE'S THE WORST OF ALL."

FOR HEAVEN'S SAKE, CHARLES. YOU'RE UPSETTING THE *CHILDREN.*

SORRY, DEAR.

ALRIGHT, MY LITTLE BEASTIES. BEDTIME.

"'E'S THE ONE THAT MORTALS ALWAYS WARNED THEIR *CHILDREN* ABOUT.

"THEY'D SAY, 'DON'T STRAY TOO NEAR THE *MARL-PIT*, OR OL' *RAWHEAD 'N' BLOODY BONES*'LL PULL YEH IN.'"

CAN I SLEEP IN YOUR ROOM TONIGHT, DADDY?

AREN'T YOU A LITTLE OLD–?

YES!

YES, YOU CAN.

"BUT *THING* 'BOUT OL' *TOMMY*, *SOMETIMES* YOU DON'T *NEED* TO GO NEAR THE *MARL-PIT* TO FIND 'IM. SOMETIMES 'E COMES *OUT*."

IS THERE *REALLY* SOMEONE OUT THERE?

A BAD PERSON?

WELL, IF THERE *WAS*, THEY'D NEVER GET IN.

YOUR *FATHER* HAS THE HOUSE UNDER HIS PROTECTION.

"AN' WHEN 'E WANTS *BLOOD*, THERE'S *NOTHIN'* CAN STOP 'IM.

"NO SPELL, NO *CURSE...*

"NO MAGIC, *HOWEVER* POWERFUL, CAN *PROTECT* YEH FROM 'IM.

"AN' IF 'E *WANTS* YEH, 'E'LL 'AVE YEH. O' *THAT YEH* CAN BE *SURE.*

"'IS ARMS IS SO *LONG*, 'E CAN *REACH* INTO THE *FURTHEST HIDIN'* PLACES.

"'IS FINGERS CAN REACH UP DRAINPIPES.

"BUT THE *FUNNIEST* THING 'BOUT 'IM, EVEN *THOUGH* 'E'S A GREAT *HUGE* BUGGER..."

"'E CAN *FIT* 'ISSELF INTO THE *TEENSIEST* PLACES."

PHEW!

DANIEL!

ELLEN, STOP!

"'E'S A *SLOPPY* EATER, TOMMY. *THINK* 'E LIKES 'IS MEALS T' *STRUGGLE* AND *SCREAM.*"

THERE'S NOTHING WE CAN DO.

GET YOUR *AMULET,* CHARLES.

WE'LL SEE HOW THIS BEAST LIKES THE TASTE OF THE FIRE AMULET.

AAAAAAAAHHH!!!

RUN, BABY.

LET THE IMMORTAL BODIES CURSE YOU, UNCLEAN THING!

KA BOOOMMM

CURSE ME?

BUT, MY LADY, I AM ALREADY ACCURS'D ONE-HUNDRED FOLD.

"NO ONE'S EVER ESCAPED OL' RAWHEAD 'N' BLOODY BONES.

"NO ONE."

HA HAHAHA HAHAHAHA HA

"NOT ONCE 'E'D MADE 'IS MIND UP T' 'AVE 'EM."

COURTNEY WATCHED THE WATERY LIGHT OF MORNING SPILL INTO THE ROOM. SHE HADN'T CLOSED HER EYES ALL NIGHT.

HER BRAIN HAD NOW ACQUIRED A THICK LINTY COAT. BUT AS AWFUL AS SHE FELT...

...SHE COULD TELL THAT UNCLE ALOYSIUS FELT WORSE.

NO HOMEWORK TODAY?

THAT *WHISTLING* YOU HEAR IS THE *FALL* OF YOUR *GRADE* POINT AVERAGE.

>SNORT<

OH, YEAH. THAT WAS *ALL KINDS* O' FUNNY, WASN'T IT?

29

MS. CRISP, CAN I CHANGE SEATS?

SURE, IF ANYONE WANTS TO TRADE.

LOOK, I WASN'T FEELING TOO GOOD LAST NIGHT.

I'M NOT GOING TO GIVE YOU A ZERO THIS TIME. I IMAGINE YOU'VE BEEN WORRYING ABOUT YOUR UNCLE.

YOU'RE A WITCH, TOO, AREN'T YOU?

TAKES YOU A WHILE, BUT YOU GET THERE IN THE END.

I'M ALSO AN OLD FRIEND OF ALOYSIUS.

THEN MAYBE YOU CAN TELL ME WHAT'S GOING ON. HE SURE AS HECK HASN'T.

HMM. PERHAPS IT'S FOR THE BEST.

THAT'S *CRAP!* IF SOMETHING MIGHT *HAPPEN* TO HIM, I NEED TO *KNOW* ABOUT IT.

HE'S *ALL* I'VE GOT.

WHY DON'T THEY JUST LEAVE HIM *ALONE?* ISN'T HE TOO *OLD* TO BE FIGHTING *MONSTERS?*

I *THOUGHT* HE HADN'T *TOLD* YOU ANYTHING.

I'VE GOT MY *SOURCES.*

I *SEE.*

IT'S NOT *FAIR!*

I *THOUGHT* HE WAS *RETIRED* OR SOMETHING. CAN'T SOMEONE *ELSE* DEAL WITH IT?

NO ONE *WANTS* TO.

ALOYSIUS WAS ALWAYS THE ONE THEY ASKED TO DO THEIR *DIRTY* WORK.

HE SAYS *"YES"* BECAUSE HE *KNOWS* IT HAS TO BE DONE.

JERKS.

THAT'S THE WAY PEOPLE ARE. DO *YOU* WANT TO GO DEAL WITH IT?

THAT'S *DIFFERENT.*

I'M A *KID.*

DO YOU THINK ANY OF *THEM* FEEL MORE QUALIFIED THAN *YOU?*

THEY *DON'T.*

COURTNEY MULLED OVER MS. CRISP'S WORDS ALL THE WAY HOME. SHE TOOK THE ROAD FOR SAFETY'S SAKE, BREAKING HER LONGTIME HABIT OF CUTTING THROUGH THE FOREST.

HEY, LOOK. FRESH MEAT.

CRUMRIN.

REMEMBER?

OH. OH YEAH.

UNCLE A?

>SNFF<

COURTNEY? WHAT'S WRONG?

NOTHING.

I WAS JUST... WORRIED.

I DON'T *WANT* YOU TO GO *OUT* TONIGHT.

MY DEAR, I *MUST*.

WHY? IT'S NOT *FAIR*.

INDEED IT *ISN'T*.

IT'S NOT FAIR THAT THE INNOCENT *SUFFER*. IT'S NOT FAIR THAT *CHILDREN DIE* AT THE HANDS OF *MONSTERS*.

IT'S NOT EVEN FAIR THAT *OLD MEN* LIKE *ME* ARE FORCED OUT OF THEIR COMFORTABLE *SITTING ROOMS* AND INTO THE COLD *NIGHT*. LIFE IS OFTEN *ENTIRELY* UNFAIR.

BUT IT BEATS THE ALTERNATIVE.

WHAT ALTERNATIVE?

EXACTLY.

I JUST HOPE WE CAN *FIND* THE BLOODY THING BEFORE IT *HURTS* ANYONE ELSE.

I DON'T THINK WE HAVE TO *WORRY* ABOUT THAT, WOODRUE.

WHY NOT?

BECAUSE SOMETHING *TELLS* ME IT'S COMING *HERE.*

HMMM...

I'LL BE BACK SOON.

HAVE A GOOD TIME.

COURTNEY DIDN'T REALLY KNOW WHAT SHE INTENDED TO DO.

SHE HAD NO PLAN, AND COULD THINK OF NO SPELLS THAT WOULD BE OF ANY USE.

BUT SHE COULDN'T SIT IN HER BED ANOTHER NIGHT KNOWING THAT HER UNCLE WAS OUT ALONE, FACING AN UNSTOPPABLE MONSTER.

PARDON, MISS.

OF COURSE, SHE HADN'T THOUGHT SHE'D BE FACING IT ALONE HERSELF.

DO YOU LIVE IN THAT HOUSE?

ME? UH...

NO. I LIVE, UH, DOWN THE STREET.

I DIDN'T JUST SEE YOU COMING OUT THE BACK DOOR OF THAT HOUSE?

THAT ONE BEHIND YOU?

OH, YEAH, THAT HOUSE. I WAS, UH, JUST VISITING.

I SEE.

YOU WOULDN'T BE LYING TO OLD TOMMY, NOW WOULD YOU?

37

HECTOR.

CREATURES LIKE *THIS* DON'T SIMPLY *APPEAR* AFTER A HUNDRED YEARS OF *BANISHMENT.*

SOMEONE *SUMMONED* THIS ONE, UNDOUBTEDLY FOR A *SPECIFIC* PURPOSE.

YOU *MIGHT* WANT TO LOOK INTO IT.

COURTNEY. IT'S A BIT CHILLY OUT.

LET'S GET INDOORS.

GENTLEMEN.

AND COURTNEY NEVER FEARED FOR UNCLE ALOYSIUS AGAIN.

Chapter Two

HOW'S MY NIECE DOING IN SCHOOL?

STILL HATES ME.

GLAD TO HEAR IT.

IF SHE DIDN'T, YOU WOULDN'T BE DOING YOUR JOB.

THIS ISN'T A JOB, ALOYSIUS.

THIS IS A FAVOR.

OF COURSE. FORGIVE ME, MY DEAR.

GOODNESS KNOWS SHE NEEDS ALL THE HELP SHE CAN GET.

I DARESAY IF I DIDN'T STEP IN, SHE'D END UP SKULKING AROUND THAT OLD HOUSE READING MOLDY BOOKS AND FRIGHTENING THE LOCAL CHILDREN.

TOTALLY USELESS WHEN IT COMES TO ANYTHING PRACTICAL.

RATHER LIKE YOU, REALLY.

YOU FLATTER ME, CALPURNIA.

NOT AT ALL.

IT'S GETTING CHILLY.

SHALL WE GRAB A CAPPUCCINO BEFORE CALLING IT A NIGHT?

MS. CRISP WAS NOT EXAGGERATING ABOUT COURTNEY'S FEELINGS TOWARD HER. IF ANYTHING, SHE UNDERSTATED THE MATTER.

WHEN SHE REALIZED JUST HOW FAR COURTNEY HAD FALLEN BEHIND IN HER STUDIES OVER THE LAST SEVERAL MONTHS, SHE BEGAN A STRICT REGIMEN TO CATCH HER STUDENT UP.

...GRUMBLE...

COURTNEY WAS BEGINNING TO LOATHE HER.

THIS ESSAY WAS *MUCH* BETTER.

I *SUSPECTED* THERE WAS AN INTELLIGENT GIRL *SOMEWHERE* UNDERNEATH THAT SCOWL.

GEE, *THANKS.*

CAN I GO YET?

AS SOON AS YOU FINISH READING THAT CHAPTER.

I'VE GOT TO RUN SOME ERRANDS. WOULD YOU *MIND* LOCKING UP *AFTER* YOURSELF?

LEAVE THE BACK DOOR **OPEN** SO QUICK CAN GET IN AND **OUT.**

IN SOME WAYS, SCHOOLWORK WASN'T MUCH DIFFERENT THAN THE STUDY OF WITCHCRAFT. HOWEVER, WITCHCRAFT, IN COURTNEY'S OPINION, HAD FAR SUPERIOR PRACTICAL VALUE, ESPECIALLY WHEN APPLIED TO HER CLASSMATES.

NOT THAT SHE MADE A HABIT OF IT, BUT HILLSBOROUGH COULD BE QUITE DULL ON A SUNDAY AFTERNOON, AND COURTNEY HAD TO GET HER ENTERTAINMENT SOMEWHERE.

WITHER.

HMMM...

DON'T EVEN **THINK** ABOUT IT, YOUNGSTER.

43

QUICK WASN'T THE FIRST TALKING CAT THAT COURTNEY HAD COME ACROSS. SHE WAS BEGINNING TO SUSPECT THAT THE NEIGHBORHOOD WAS FULL OF THEM. SHE WASN'T EXACTLY AN ANIMAL PERSON, AND REGARDED CATS AS TCHOTCHKES THAT WALKED ABOUT.

BUT SHE WAS AN INQUISITIVE GIRL, AS I'VE MENTIONED BEFORE, AND HER CURIOSITY WAS PIQUED.

WHETHER A CAT CAN TALK OR NOT IS THE CAT'S BUSINESS.

IT'S NOT FOR ME TO TELL, UNLESS THE CAT IS MYSELF.

WHAT'S THE DEAL ANYWAY?

CAN ALL CATS TALK, OR WAS THERE SOME RADIATION LEAKAGE AROUND HERE OR SOMETHING?

UH-HUH. WHAT I GET FOR ASKING A CAT.

YOU CATCH ON FAST.

QUICK!

THERE YOU ARE.

WHAT'S THE HOLD-UP, GIRL? WE HAVE BUSINESS.

AH.

HELLO, MISS CRUMRIN.

HEY, BOO. WHERE ARE YOU GUYS OFF TO?

NONE OF YOUR BUSINESS.

ACTUALLY, YOU MIGHT FIND THIS INTERESTING. COME WITH US.

YOU MUST *EAT* OF THE *PLANT* THAT GROWS IN THE *SHADOW* OF THIS TREE.

BUT *BEFORE* WE COME TO THE GATHERING, THERE'S SOMETHING YOU MUST DO, MISS CRUMRIN.

IS THERE?

HMPH. *JUST THAT?* WHY?

I DO *NOT ASK* LIGHTLY.

I CERTAINLY HAVE NO *LIKING* FOR *BRIAR* AND *BRACKEN,* THE *FOOD* OF MY PREY.

BUT *THIS* YOU *MUST* DO, OR GO HOME.

IT WAS AN ODD REQUEST, BUT COURTNEY WAS BY NOW FILLED WITH CURIOSITY FOR WHAT LAY AHEAD.

MISS CRUMRIN, IS *THAT* A PLANT?

HUH?

THAT'S A *FUNGUS.* IT'S QUITE POTENT, BUT I DON'T THINK YOU'D *BENEFIT* FROM ITS PROPERTIES.

I *THINK* I'LL ASK MS. CALPURNIA TO ADD BOTANY TO YOUR CURRICULUM.

46

WHAT DOES IT DO?

IT ANIMATES THE DEAD.

BLEAGH!

IS THIS IT?

YES.

WHAT DOES IT DO?

IT WILL ENABLE YOU TO WITNESS OUR SECRET COUNCIL.

IT GIVES ME NIGHT VISION?

AMONG OTHER THINGS.

OKAY, BOO. I'LL TRUST YOU THIS TIME.

COME ON, LET'S GET GOING.

AND SO THE THREE OF THEM DEPARTED FROM THE CLEARING AND PLUNGED INTO THE DARKNESS OF THE WOOD.

YEAH, I THINK I CAN SEE A BIT BETTER.

OW!

WATCH OUT FOR THOSE TREE ROOTS, YOUNGSTER.

I DON'T KNOW HOW YOU TWO-LEGGED CREATURES MANAGE.

WHERE ARE THE *OTHER* CATS?

I THOUGHT YOU SAID IT WAS A *MEETING* OR A *COUNCIL* OR SOMETHING.

USE YOUR *EYES*.

THEY'RE ALL *AROUND* YOU.

COURTNEY FELT THE HACKLES ON THE BACK OF HER NECK RISE. THE NIGHT WAS ALIVE WITH THE FIERCE GAZE OF HUNTERS.

THEY'RE *HUGE*.

NO, CHILD. YOU'VE *SHED* A BIT OF UNNECESSARY *WEIGHT*.

WHAT!!! OH, YOU GOTTA BE KIDDING...

QUIET, GIRL.

DON'T *WORRY*. YOUR LARGE, LUMBERING FORM WILL RETURN IN THE *MORNING*.

FOR *NOW*, KEEP SILENT. *MORTALS* ARE FORBIDDEN HERE.

50

I HAVE FULFILLED THE DUTIES AND REAPED THE PROFITS OF LEADERSHIP FOR TWENTY WINTERS.

LAST NIGHT, AS WAS MY DUTY, I FACED DOWN AND SLEW THE HOUND OF RADLEY HALL.

IT WAS A COSTLY VICTORY.

AS ONE, THE GATHERED ANIMALS LOWERED THEIR HEADS IN RESPECTFUL SADNESS.

EXCEPT ONE.

A LEADER MUST LEAD BY EXAMPLE.

HE MUST BE THE GREATEST HUNTER AMONG US.

UNTIL YESTERDAY, I HELD THAT DISTINCTION.

BUT A HUNTER NEEDS TWO GOOD EYES, AND I SHALL ONLY EVER SEE AGAIN OUT OF ONE.

TONIGHT, YOU MUST SELECT A NEW LEADER.

SUDDENLY THE LABYRINTHINE BRANCHES WERE ALIVE WITH THE WHISPERINGS OF CATS. THE SOUND CHILLED COURTNEY TO THE BONES. ONE WORD SEEMED TO ECHO THROUGH THE ASSEMBLY.

MITTENS.

MITTENS, GRAY AS MOONLIGHT, WHICH SEEMED TO PASS THROUGH HIM, LEAVING HIM ALMOST INVISIBLE, BUT FOR HIS WHITE PAWS.

IT'S GOING TO BE A *CLOSE THING.* BOO IS WELL REGARDED, BUT *MITTENS* IS DEADLY.

DEADLIER THAN I, THOUGH I'M FAST AS MY NAME.

PERHAPS.

PERHAPS DEADLIER THAN BOO.

COURTNEY TRIED AGAIN TO PICK HIM OUT OF THE DARKNESS.

CERTAINLY QUIETER.

WE SHALL SEE.

INDEED.

A MEMBER OF *YOUR* PRIDE, QUICK?

YES. COURTNEY IS HER NAME.

A STRANGE ODOR.

NOT UNPLEASANT. BUT *UNUSUAL* TO BE *SURE.* ALMOST...

SILENCE.

TOBERMORY SPEAKS.

THE HUNT BEGINS TONIGHT. YOU, WHO WOULD BE LEADER, MUST KNOW THAT TO RULE A *SINGLE CAT,* MUCH LESS ALL CATS, IS AN IMPOSSIBLE TASK.

THEREFORE, YOU MUST *SHOW* US THAT YOU ARE *EQUAL* TO IT BY HUNTING THE *UNCATCHABLE* PREY.

WERE IT UP TO ME, I'D NAME HIM AS MY SUCCESSOR.

BUT LEADERSHIP MUST BE EARNED. IT'S THE ONLY WAY TO PRESERVE THE RESPECT OF OUR KIND.

DO YOU THINK HE'LL WIN?

I'VE SEEN MANY SKILLED HUNTERS IN MY NIGHTS UPON THIS EARTH. BOO IS ONE OF THE BEST.

HE WOULD MAKE A GREAT LEADER.

BUT HE WILL NOT WIN.

YOU THINK MITTENS'LL BEAT HIM?

MITTENS IS DEADLY.

I'M SADDENED, FOR ALL WILL SUFFER UNDER HIS RULE.

HE IS COLD AND CRUEL, MORE SO THAN IS GOOD EVEN FOR A CAT.

THAT SUCKS.

INDEED.

BUT YOU CAME HERE TO WATCH, YOU SAID.

YOU'D BETTER MOVE FAST, OR YOU'LL SEE NOTHING, AND YOUR JOURNEY WILL BE IN VAIN.

SUDDENLY COURTNEY FOUND HERSELF PLUMMETING TO THE EARTH. IN A PANIC SHE TWISTED ROUND TO SEE THE GROUND COMING UP TOWARD HER.

HUH.

COOL.

WITH HER CAT EYES, SHE SAW THE FOREST ANEW. EACH RAY OF THE MOON ILLUMINATED THE TREES WITH A FROSTY BRILLIANCE. OF THE OTHER CATS THERE WAS NO SIGN.

YET SOMETHING PROPELLED HER FORWARD; A COMPELLING SENSE WHICH LED TO BOO.

WHEN SHE FOUND HIM, HER NEWLY ACQUIRED INSTINCTS HELD HER SILENT. HE WAS PREPARING TO SPRING.

HIS PREY MUST HAVE BEEN CLOSE, BUT SHE COULDN'T AS YET SEE IT.

TRUE. I SHALL NOT FORGET AGAIN.

THEN HE MELTED INTO THE NIGHT.

YOU OKAY?

YES, BUT NOW HE'LL MORE EASILY SMELL MY COMING.

SHOULDN'T YOU BE TRYING TO CATCH THE THING YOURSELF?

PERHAPS. I CERTAINLY SHOULDN'T BE SITTING HERE LICKING MY WOUNDS.

FAREWELL.

BOO SLIPPED LIKE A SHADOW INTO THE DARKNESS, LEAVING COURTNEY ALONE ONCE AGAIN.

JUST AS SHE RESOLVED TO FOLLOW, SHE HEARD STRANGE NOISES.

THE FOREST, THOUGH ALIVE WITH CATS DASHING BACK AND FORTH, NEVER VISIBLE FOR MORE THAN A SECOND, HAD BEEN SILENT UP TILL NOW.

SUCH A TERRIFIC CLAMOR SHATTERED THE SILENCE THAT SHE WAS CONVINCED A BULLDOZER WAS MOVING THROUGH THE TREES.

THEN SHE HEARD VOICES.

HUMAN VOICES.

THERE. DO YOU SEE THE TRACK?

THE BEAST CAN'T BE FAR. THE UNDERBRUSH IS STILL MOVING.

COURTNEY TRIED TO SUPPRESS HERSELF, BUT BY THEN HER NERVES WERE ON EDGE.

RAERRRR!

WAS THAT *IT*?

NO, BUT I'LL WAGER IT'S NEAR.

THERE.

THE FOREST IS *FULL* OF CATS TONIGHT, BUT *THAT'S* THE FIRST ONE I'VE *HEARD*.

SOMETHING *STARTLED* IT.

THE HUGE MEN CRASH OFF THROUGH THE BUSHES LIKE ELEPHANTS. COURTNEY KNEW THAT SHE'D LEAD THEM RIGHT TO THEIR QUARRY, AND DIDN'T FEEL GOOD ABOUT IT. HER INQUISITIVENESS UNQUENCHED, SHE RESOLVED TO FOLLOW.

,Snap,

WHAT WAS THAT!?!

IT'S THAT KITTEN AGAIN.

GONE. BLAST IT.

THEY CRASHED AWAY AGAIN.

)SCRITCH
)SCRITCH

COURTNEY WENT RIGID AS SHE TURNED TO MEET THE GAZE OF THE CREATURE. WHAT SHE SAW IN ITS EYES GAVE HER PAUSE.

THEN IT DEFTLY PLUNGED BACK INTO THE FOREST.

COURTNEY WAS QUITE ASTOUNDED. SHE'D MET MANY CREATURES OF THE NIGHT, BEFRIENDED A FEW, BEEN CHARMED BY SOME, REPELLED BY OTHERS. SHE'D NEVER REALLY CONSIDERED BEFORE WHETHER ANY OF THEM HAD A SOUL.

LOOKING INTO THIS ONE'S EYES, SHE HAD NO DOUBT.

FILLED WITH WONDER, SHE DETERMINED TO MEET IT AGAIN.

ITS SCENT WAS SWEET AND MUSKY IN HER NOSTRILS, AND BEFORE LONG SHE FOUND IT...

...CROUCHING BY A CLEAR STREAM TO QUENCH ITS THIRST.

THEN SHE HEARD THE DREADFUL SOUND OF A HUMAN VOICE.

GOT YOU NOW, YOU FOUL THING.

COURTNEY KNEW SHE HAD LESS THAN A SECOND TO ACT. SHE TURNED AND DASHED AT THE HUNTER, LEAPING TO THE ATTACK.

EHEM.

PROFESSOR!?!

WHAT ARE YOU DOING HERE?

I MIGHT ASK YOU THE SAME QUESTION.

RATHER UNSPORTSMANLIKE CHOICE OF QUARRY, DON'T YOU THINK?

I'M SO SORRY, PROFESSOR. I WAS HUNTING—

I KNOW WHAT YOU WERE HUNTING.

I THINK YOU SHOULD GO HOME NOW.

BUT PROFESSOR...

YES, SIR.

AND YOU TOO, YOUNG LADY.

IT'S PAST YOUR BEDTIME.

WHEN COURTNEY RETURNED TO THE TREE, THE CATS HAD GATHERED AGAIN. BOO LAY IN A CORNER, LICKING MANY WOUNDS.

ARE YOU ALL RIGHT?

THE CLAW THAT DOES NOT SLAY ME STRENGTHENS ME.

DID YOU CATCH IT? THE WILL-O-THINGY?

NO.

MITTENS.

A GREAT HUNTER. BETTER THAN I.

HE TRACKED HIS PREY AS I NEVER COULD.

YET HE'S NOT AS WISE AS SOME AMONG US. HE FORGOT, OR NEVER LEARNED, THAT THE ELVEN FIRE LURES THOSE WHO SEEK IT TO THEIR DOOM.

MITTENS SANK INTO THE MARL-PIT.

65

A HUNTER MUST BE WISE IN THE WAYS OF HIS PREY.

I'LL NOT FORGET, TOBERMORY.

SO YOU STILL DON'T HAVE A LEADER.

OH, WE DO. THE WORTHIEST AMONG US.

CERTAINLY THE FASTEST.

AND PERHAPS THE WISEST.

QUICK LOOKED DOWN AT COURTNEY WITH A SATISFIED EXPRESSION.

IN HER PAWS, STILL STRUGGLING, WAS A CURIOUS CREATURE, SUCH AS COURTNEY HAD NEVER SEEN BEFORE.

OH BUGGER.

SURE GLAD IT'S SATURDAY.

"NOW I'M GONNA GET IT," SHE THOUGHT, IMAGINING THE HUNDRED DANGEROUS THINGS SHE DID THAT NIGHT.

COURTNEY. COME *THIS* WAY, PLEASE.

ARE YOU *MAD* AT ME?

NOT AT ALL.

RATHER IMPRESSED, ACTUALLY.

BUT THERE'S *SOMEONE* HERE WHO'D LIKE TO THANK YOU *PROPERLY* FOR YOUR *BRAVERY* LAST NIGHT.

WHAT ARE YOU *TALKING* ABOUT—

OH.

COURTNEY, THIS IS *SKARROW*.

HE'LL BE STAYING AS MY *GUEST* FOR A WHILE.

UH... HI.

Chapter Three

MADAM HARKEN'S GARDEN WAS OVERGROWN EVEN BY HILLSBOROUGH STANDARDS, AND THAT'S SAYING SOMETHING.

BUT THEN, AS YOU MAY HAVE HEARD, SHE WASN'T THE SORT OF WITCH WHO STROVE TO KEEP UP APPEARANCES.

I CALLED YOU *ROUND* AS SOON AS I'D *HEARD*, PROFESSOR.

YOU KNOW HER BEST.

PERHAPS. YEARS AGO.

THE HOUSE WAS DARK AND DISHEVELED; BOOKS CLUTTERED THE SHELVES, KNICK-KNACKS OBSESSIVELY COLLECTED ON EVERY SURFACE.

DUST COATED EVERYTHING.

MADAM *HARKEN?*

71

PROFESSOR!

COUNCILMAN!

THIS WAY.

slam

MADAM HARKEN?

HERMIA.

WHAT'S HAPPENED?

Bleargh

STRANGE.

SHE HAD SUCH PROMISE. A GREAT FAMILY, THE HARKENS.

HOW SHE CAME TO THIS...

WHAT EXACTLY DO YOU THINK HAPPENED HERE, WOODRUE?

IT'S NOT TOO HARD TO GUESS.

MADAM HERMIA'S LITTLE "MINION" TURNED ON HER AT LAST.

INEVITABLE, IF YOU ASK ME.

BUT HECTOR WILL TRACK IT DOWN.

I SERIOUSLY DOUBT THAT.

WHY?

BECAUSE I HAVE THE CREATURE UNDER MY PROTECTION.

YOU WHAT!?!

THE TWO WARLOCKS WERE INTERRUPTED BY THE SOUNDS OF COMMOTION FROM THE FRONT YARD.

OH DEAR.

WORD'S GOTTEN OUT.

LADIES AND GENTLEMEN, EVERYTHING IS IN HAND HERE.

PLEASE DON'T BE ALARMED.

WHERE'S MISS HARKEN!?!

WHAT'S HAPPENING?

WHAT ARE YOU GOING TO DO ABOUT IT!?

PLEASE, PEOPLE! LET US THROUGH.

IN TRUTH, NO WITCH OR WARLOCK HAD EVEN SEEN MADAM HARKEN IN YEARS, AND MOST HAD NEVER SEEN HER UP CLOSE.

GOOD HEAVENS, LOOK AT HER.

BREATHTAKING!

HASN'T AGED A DAY.

COURTNEY?

MMM, HUH?

OH, HEY, UNCLE A.

SORRY TO DISTURB YOU. I JUST WANTED TO SEE THAT YOU WERE ALL RIGHT.

YEAH. WE'RE COOL.

I ALWAYS WONDERED IF YOU HAD TEETH. GOOD TO KNOW.

HOW ABOUT SOME BREAKFAST?

IT'S WEIRD. IT'S LIKE I JUST KNOW WHAT HE MEANS.

HE DOESN'T HAVE TO SAY ANYTHING.

I KNOW.

WHY WERE THOSE **MEN** TRYING TO **KILL** HIM LAST NIGHT?

THEY BELIEVE HE **DID** SOMETHING...

...SOMETHING EXTREMELY CRUEL, TO A **WITCH**.

WHAT?

A CURSE.

DID HE?

WHAT DO **YOU** THINK?

NO WAY.

I DUNNO, HE'S... HE'S LIKE A BIG PUPPY.

HE'S TOO **SWEET** TO DO ANYTHING MEAN TO ANYBODY. YA **KNOW?**

I DO.

KRÓÓK!

WHAT WAS THAT?

STAY HERE.

NOW YOU PEOPLE STAY OUTSIDE. THIS IS COUNCIL BUSINESS.

GENTLEMEN, PLEASE—

HE THINKS HE CAN JUST DO WHAT HE LIKES!

HE'S NOT GETTING AWAY WITH IT!

WE'RE GOING TO SEE THAT MONSTER DEAD, YOU HEAR ME!

CAN I HELP YOU PEOPLE?

UH...

SEE HERE, CRUMRIN.

YOU'D BETTER DELIVER THAT BEAST OVER TO US.

HAD I?

OR THERE'LL BE TROUBLE IN THIS HOUSE, I CAN TELL YOU...

NOW, JOSEPH—

WILL THERE?

SEEMS TO ME YOU'RE ALL TRESPASSING.

HECTOR IS MY WITNESS. I'VE EVERY RIGHT TO REDUCE YOU ALL TO SOOT—

WHAT'S GOING ON?

COURTNEY! GO BACK UPSTAIRS. EVERYTHING'S FINE.

WHO ARE YOU GUYS?

WE'RE... WE'RE...

WHAT THE DEVIL IS GOING ON HERE?

HECTOR, DID YOU LET THESE PEOPLE INSIDE?

I COULDN'T STOP THEM, SIR. THEY WANT AN EXPLANATION.

THAT'S *RIGHT.* WHO'S IN *AUTHORITY* HERE? THE *COUNCIL,* OR *ALOYSIUS CRUMRIN?*

ALRIGHT, FOLKS, YOU'VE MADE YOUR POINT.

GO *HOME* AND LET US HANDLE THIS.

THE CROWD BEGRUDGINGLY ALLOWED ITSELF TO BE USHERED OUT OF THE HOUSE. COURTNEY WATCHED THEM GO, HER OPINION OF WITCH SOCIETY DROPPING BY THE SECOND.

YOUNG LADY, THAT WAS A *VERY* FOOLISH THING TO DO.

STOPPED 'EM, DIDN'T IT?

I HAD MATTERS WELL IN HAND. YOU COULD HAVE BEEN *SERIOUSLY HURT.*

THEY MAY BE *WITCHES,* BUT THEY'RE *STILL* PEOPLE.

STUPID, SELF-ABSORBED, REACTIONARY PEOPLE.

80

GLAD TO SEE THAT YOU HOLD SUCH A *HIGH OPINION* OF OUR *PEERS*.

YOUR PEERS, WOODRUE.

ALOYSIUS, WE'RE *HERE* TO TAKE THIS CREATURE PRISONER.

ARE YOU GOING TO STAND IN THE WAY OF THE *COUNCIL?*

YOU'RE NOT THE COUNCIL, AND NEITHER IS *HECTOR*.

YOU'LL HAVE TO HOLD A *COUNCIL SESSION* AND *PROVE YOUR CLAIM* BEFORE I ALLOW YOU ANYWHERE *NEAR* HIM.

DAMN YOU AND YOUR *STIFF NECK*, CRUMRIN—

HE'S *RIGHT*, SIR.

TECHNICALLY THE CREATURE IS HIS *PROPERTY*, AND AS *LAWKEEPERS*, WE HAVE TO *PROVE OUR CLAIM* TO IT.

FOR GOODNESS' SAKE, ALOYSIUS, YOU SAW WHAT IT DID TO THAT *WOMAN*. SHE WAS YOUR *STUDENT*.

AREN'T YOU *OUTRAGED?* HAVE YOU NO HEART?

MY HEART'S WORKING *FINE*, AND SO IS MY BRAIN.

WHAT POSSIBLE REASON COULD THIS CREATURE HAVE TO *CAST* SUCH A CURSE, CLEARLY INTENDED TO *SILENCE* ITS VICTIM?

OBVIOUSLY SO SHE COULDN'T TELL WHAT *ELSE* HE MIGHT HAVE DONE.

AH, YES. HOW CLEVER.

THE LIKELIEST SUSPECT OF THE CRIME COMMITTED IT PRECISELY IN ORDER TO SHIELD HIMSELF FROM BLAME.

NOW, ALOYSIUS, ARE YOU QUESTIONING OUR MARSHAL'S DETECTIVE WORK?

I MIGHT, WERE HE TO DO ANY.

I'LL SEE YOU TWO AT THE COUNCIL SESSION.

THAT IS, IF YOU CAN ASSEMBLE ENOUGH NONSENSE TO HOLD ONE.

PLEASE DON'T HESITATE TO GET OUT.

COURTNEY?

YEAH?

K-KLAK

I FORBID YOU TO INVOLVE YOURSELF IN THIS MATTER.

I MEAN IT.

YES, SIR.

WHAT DO YOU KNOW ABOUT *SKARROW*?

THEY SAY 'E WERE ONCE A *MORTAL CHILD* TAKEN BY THE *KINDLY ONES* YEARS AGO.

TILL *YESTERDAY*, HE LIVED WITH OL' MADAM *HARKEN*, YONDER.

HARKEN. WHAT'S *HER* DEAL?

YOU SHOULD *KNOW*, MISSY. YOUR *UNCLE* TAUGHT HER.

ALWAYS ONE FOR STUDYIN' US *NIGHT THINGS*, MISS HARKEN.

CAUGHT ME IN THE *WOODS* COUPLE O' TIMES, WHEN SHE WERE A LASS. BUT SHE WERE *MUCH* NICER 'N YOU.

THINK I'D *BETTER* HAVE A *LOOK* AT HER.

GONNA BE *HARD* TE DO *THAT.* THEM *WARLOCKS* 'AVE 'ER UP AT *RADLEY HALL.*

NOBODY GETS IN *THERE* UNLESS THEY *LET* 'EM.

THAT *SO?*

A *FIELD* TRIP?

IT'S JUST THAT YOU'RE ALWAYS *SAYING* I NEED TO LEARN ABOUT *PRACTICAL* THINGS.

IF *I'M* GOING TO BE PART OF THIS, YA KNOW, *COVEN,* OR *WHATEVER,* I SHOULD KNOW SOMETHING *ABOUT* IT.

THAT'S PRACTICAL, *ISN'T* IT?

EXTREMELY SO.

TELL YOU *WHAT.* YOU *KNOW* THAT CREATIVE *WRITING* PROJECT YOU WERE PLANNING ON *NOT DOING?*

I WAS GOING TO—

UH HUH.

OKAY, I'LL DO IT.

AND *READ* IT IN FRONT OF *CLASS, JUST* LIKE EVERYONE *ELSE.*

YES, MS. CRISP.

RADLEY HALL WAS ONE OF THOSE BIG BLANK BUILDINGS WITH NO OBVIOUS SIGN OR LABEL, AND ONE NEVER SEES ANYONE ENTER OR LEAVE. IT WAS THE SORT OF BUILDING THAT ONE SIMPLY IGNORES, BECAUSE IT'S BEEN THERE SINCE BEFORE ANYONE CAN REMEMBER.

COURTNEY HAD PASSED THE PLACE EVERY DAY ON HER WALK TO SCHOOL, YET IT NEVER OCCURRED TO HER TO WONDER WHO USED IT, AND FOR WHAT PURPOSE.

JUST TAKING MY *STUDENT* ON A TOUR. WE WON'T *DISTURB* ANYONE. SHE WANTS TO SEE THE *HALL* OF WONDERS.

NAMES?

MS. CRISP, AND MISS CRUMRIN.

WHAT'S THE *HALL* OF WONDERS?

YOU'LL SEE.

CALPURNIA?

HECTOR. IT'S BEEN A *WHILE.*

YES INDEED. WHAT BRINGS YOU TO THIS *FUSTY* OLD *RUIN?*

MY *STUDENT.* COURTNEY, THIS IS—

BUT OF *COURSE* I KNOW MISS CRUMRIN.

I SEE YOUR *UNCLE* ISN'T THE ONLY WICKED INFLUENCE ON YOU.

JUST TRYING TO KEEP HER *FEET* ON THE *GROUND.*

TO BE *SURE.* QUITE A CHALLENGE WITH THE PROFESSOR AROUND, I DARE SAY.

WHILE WE'RE ON THE *SUBJECT,* THERE'S *SOMETHING* I'D LIKE TO *TALK* TO YOU ABOUT.

WOULD YOU *EXCUSE* US, MISS CRUMRIN?

THE HALL OF WONDERS FAR EXCEEDED ITS TITLE. COURTNEY HAD SEEN MANY AMAZING THINGS, BUT NOTHING SO MARVELOUS AS THE ARTIFACTS DISPLAYED HEREIN.

SHE WANDERED WIDE-EYED THROUGH THE EXHIBITS...

...UNTIL SHE CAME UPON AN UNPLEASANTLY FAMILIAR FACE.

RAWHEAD AND BLOODY BONES
~ Destroyed by the Council of Elders ~

YEAH RIGHT. DESTROYED BY COMMITTEE.

SUDDENLY, THOUGH SHE COULDN'T SAY WHY, COURTNEY KNEW SHE WAS BEING WATCHED.

YOU'VE GOOD EYES FOR A MORTAL.

I'VE NEVER BEEN SPOTTED BEFORE.

TOBERMORY?

I THOUGHT YOU SMELT FAMILIAR, THOUGH YOU'VE PUT ON SOME WEIGHT SINCE WE LAST MET.

AND LOST A BIT OF FUR. HOW DID YOU GET IN?

I HAVE MY METHODS. IT'S BEST TO KEEP AN EYE ON YOU MORTALS.

THERE YOU ARE.

PRETTY AMFUL, HUH?

THOUGH I GATHER THIS ISN'T YOUR *FIRST CLOSE LOOK.*

HMMM. WHAT'D THE COP WANT?

HECTOR? OH, NOTHING IMPORTANT.

WAS IT ABOUT MY UNCLE?

WHAT MAKES YOU THINK *THAT?*

I GOT MY SOURCES.

SO I'VE GATHERED.

YES, HE WANTED ME TO *TALK* WITH ALOYSIUS. AND I WILL.

WHAT ARE YOU GOING TO SAY?

JUST TO BE *CAREFUL* HOW HE HANDLES THE COUNCIL.

YOUR *UNCLE* HAS ALIENATED A *LOT* OF PEOPLE OVER THE YEARS.

THAT'S *NOT* ALWAYS SUCH A WISE WAY TO LIVE.

HE SEEMS TO DO OKAY. NOBODY *MESSES* WITH HIM.

ISOLATION ISN'T EVERYTHING.

IT'S NOT *WISE* TO TURN YOUR *BACK* ON THE WORLD.

COURTNEY DIDN'T CARE FOR MS. CRISP AT ALL, BUT SHE KNEW THAT HER TEACHER WAS NO FOOL. SHE WEIGHED THOSE LAST WORDS THOUGHTFULLY AS SHE WALKED HOME.

I DON'T HAVE ANY MORE MONEY.

BETTER GET YOUR *PARENTS* TO UP YOUR *ALLOWANCE.* YOU'RE GOING TO *NEED* IT.

"THE WORLD CAN BE A PRETTY SUCKY PLACE," THOUGHT COURTNEY. "SMALL WONDER UNCLE ALOYSIUS DOESN'T GET TOO INVOLVED IN IT."

WORKING ON THE *CASE?*

BRUSHING *UP* ON THE *ARCHAIC LAWS* REGARDING SKARROW'S *KIND.*

WARLOCKS HAVE *NEVER* TRUSTED THE NIGHT THINGS.

WHY *NOT?*

WITCHCRAFT CAME INTO BEING *PARTIALLY* TO *COUNTER* THE CREATURES OF THE UNDERWORLD.

IN OLDEN TIMES THEY WERE BLAMED FOR *EVERYTHING* FROM *ECLIPSES* TO *TOOTHACHES.*

I'M AFRAID THE PREJUDICE HAS *STUCK* THROUGHOUT THE AGES, DESPITE *CENTURIES* OF *RESEARCH.* PEOPLE LIKE *WOODRUE* WOULD STILL USE THEM AS *SCAPEGOATS* FOR ALL THE WORLD'S SORROWS.

BUT YOU WON'T LET THEM *HURT HIM, WILL* YOU?

I'LL *CERTAINLY* DO MY *BEST,* MY DEAR.

I'VE BEEN *THINKING.* SKARROW DIDN'T CAST THAT CURSE, *RIGHT?*

SO WHO *DID?*

GOOD *QUESTION.*

UNFORTUNATELY, THE ONLY PERSON WHO MIGHT *KNOW* CANNOT TELL US.

"WE'LL SEE ABOUT THAT," THOUGHT COURTNEY.

MISSY? THAT YOU?

YEAH. WHO'S THE RUNT?

ME LITTLE BROTHER, BUTTERBUG.

RUH!

WHAT'D YOU BRING HIM FOR? COULDN'T FIND A BABYSITTER?

TOUGH JOB, RADLEY HALL... THOUGHT YE COULD USE THE HELP.

SHOULDN'T BE TOO HARD. I HAVE AN INSIDE MAN.

THIS WAY.

ISN'T THERE A HUGE, SLAVERING MASTIFF THAT PROTECTS THE GROUNDS?

THERE USED TO BE.

BREAK IN A *LOT*, DO YA?

I'VE BEEN KEEPING AN *EYE* ON THIS AFFAIR FOR *WEEKS*, EVER SINCE THE *HOBGOBLIN* EMERGED FROM ITS LONG *BANISHMENT*.

SOMETHING AROUND HERE SMELLS EVEN *WORSE* THAN *HE* DID.

AS RAY OF MOONLIGHT PIERCES *GLASS*, SO SHALL TOBERMORY PASS.

TAKE *NOTE*, MISS CRUMRIN.

IT'S MUCH SIMPLER TO *TRICK* A SPELL THAN TO *BREAK* IT.

WARLOCKS ALWAYS DO IT THE *HARD* WAY.

THIS IS WHERE I LEAVE *YOU*. I'VE BUSINESS OF MY OWN.

COOL. THANKS FOR THE *HELP*.

THIS MUST BE *HECTOR'S* OFFICE.

LOOKS LIKE AN *INCIDENT* REPORT FOR LAST *NIGHT*.

'R SOMETHING.

HMMM...

MADAM *HARKEN* MUST BE THROUGH THERE.

92

HERE, TAKE THIS PEN.

CAN YOU WRITE?

DO YOU SEE THAT, SIR?

DIABOLICAL.

NO, NOT HER. THERE'S SOMEONE ELSE I NEED TO TALK TO. DOWNSTAIRS.

THERE.

FER GOODNESS' SAKE, MISS. YE'VE GOT TE BE JOKIN'!

WHY 'IM?

CALL IT A HUNCH. JUST HELP ME.

YER A CRUMRIN ALRIGHT. NERVES OF IRON.

GRUH!

CAN'T HE TALK?

NEVER COULD TEACH 'IM MORTAL SPEECH. 'IS TONGUE'S TOO BIG.

WELL, YOU BETTER SHUT HIM UP OR WE'RE ALL IN FOR IT.

GRAH! GRAH!

WOULD YOU SHUT-

-OH BUGGER.

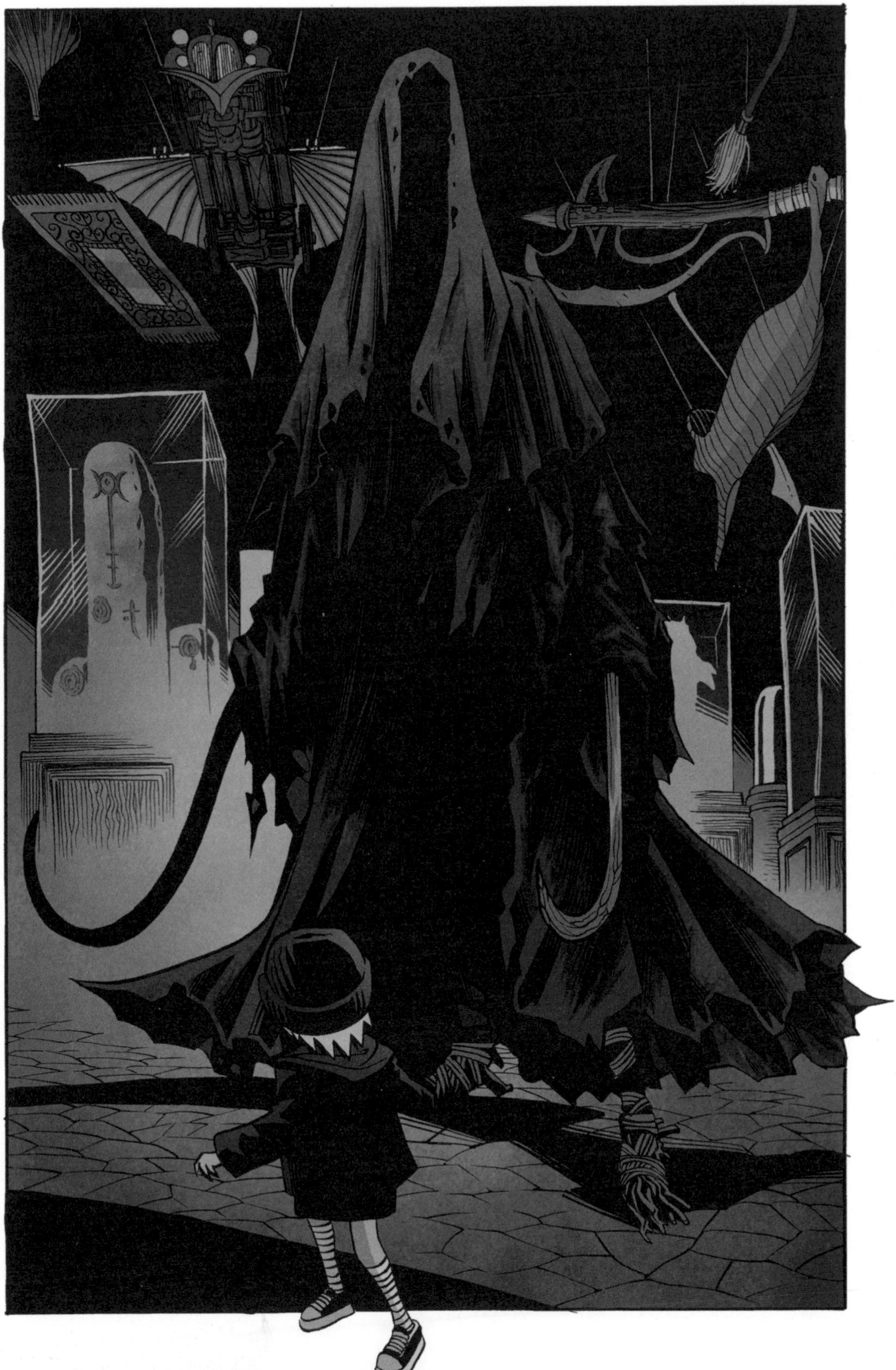

WOOOSSSSHHH

I THORT THE EXIT WOULD BE BEST, LASS.

WHERE ARE YOU GOING!?!

BUT YOU'LL TRIP THE ALARMS!

I THINK THEY'RE TRIPPED, MISS SMARTY- PANTS!

GRAH!!!

SKREEEEEEEEE

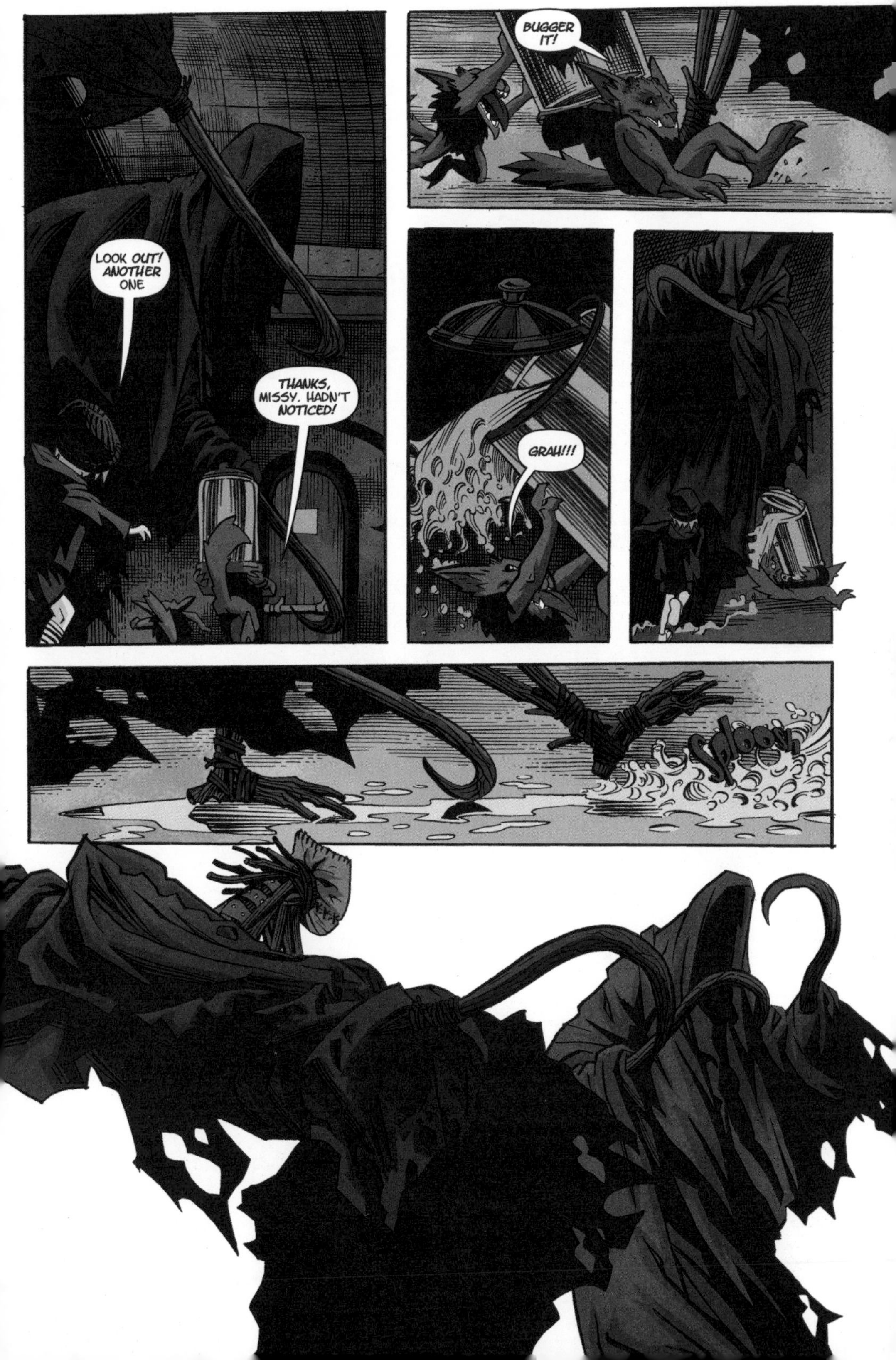
LOOK OUT! ANOTHER ONE
THANKS, MISSY. HADN'T NOTICED!
BUGGER IT!
GRAH!!!
SPLOOSH

CRASSSSHHH!

KEEP DOOR
CLOSED AT
ALL TIMES

KEEP DOOR
CLOSED AT
ALL TIMES

Snap

Chapter Four

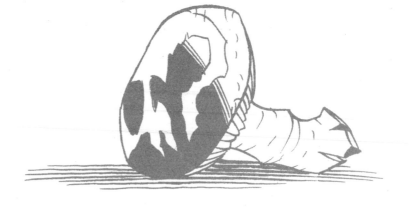

THE JAUNDICE ROOT, PLEASE.

SIX SHILLINGS.

OW, HEY!

A MORTAL! A MORTAL!

MIND YOUR OWN BUSINESS, FUZZY!

ANYBODY ELSE WANT SOME O' THIS!?!

WHAT UNDER *EARTH* IS GOING ON?

THIS *MORTAL* ATTACKED ME, YOUR *DREADFULNESS.*

YOU BETTER *BELIEVE* IT, PAL.

BACK OFF UNLESS YOU WANT *ANOTHER* ONE!

BRING HER TO ME.

HAH! SERVES YOU *RIGHT,* MORTAL. I'M AN *IMPORTANT GOBLIN* AROUND HERE.

COURTNEY CONSIDERED MAKING A RUN FOR IT, BUT THE APPROACHING CREATURE'S POWERFUL SINEWS AND SHARP CLAWS TESTIFIED TO THE FUTILITY OF THE IDEA.

MY UNCLE WON'T LIKE THIS.

HONESTLY, MY DEAR. SUCH CHILDISH THREATS ARE *BENEATH* - YOU.

JAUNDICE ROOT.

BLACK BELLADONNA.

SALAMANDER BILE.

I KNOW ALOYSIUS CRUMRIN WELL ENOUGH TO *GUESS* THAT THIS ISN'T *HIS* SHOPPING LIST.

NECROMANCY ISN'T HIS *STYLE*.

A LITTLE HOBBY OF YOUR *OWN?*

WHAT'S IT TO YOU?

NOTHING. HUMAN AFFAIRS ARE ALL *ONE* TO ME.

SO *LONG* AS THEY DON'T INVOLVE MY *PEOPLE*.

YOU HAVEN'T HEARD ABOUT THE *TRIAL*, THEN? ABOUT *SKARROW?*

I'VE *HEARD*, CHILD.

I'M TRYING TO *HELP* HIM.

SEE, A *LOT OF WEIRD STUFF* HAS BEEN HAPPENING.

IT DOESN'T TAKE A *GENIUS* TO GUESS THAT WHOEVER *SUMMONED* THAT MONSTER A FEW WEEKS AGO, THAT *TOMMY* THE BLOODY BONEHEAD, YA KNOW, PROBABLY DID THE *CURSE* ON THE *WITCH*-CHICK.

I DON'T *KNOW*. 'CAUSE I *LIKE* HIM, I GUESS.

I *FIGURE* HE'S GOT SOME MAGICAL *AURA*, LIKE A *GLAMOUR* SPELL. I'M NOT *STUPID*, I'VE *NOTICED*. BUT EVEN SO, IT'S NOT FAIR TO *BLAME* HIM FOR OTHER PEOPLE'S CRAP.

WHY DO *YOU* CARE WHAT HAPPENS TO A *NIGHT THING*?

I SEE.

HE'S ONE OF YOUR *PEOPLE*, ISN'T HE? YOU'RE A BIG SHOT DOWN HERE. CAN'T *YOU* HELP?

HE'S MORE THAN MY *PEOPLE*, HE'S MY *CHILD*.

WHAT!?!

CENTURIES AGO, HE WAS A *HUMAN* BOY.

I TOOK HIM AS MY *OWN*, AND LEFT A *CHANGELING* IN HIS *PLACE*.

BUT AT LAST HE *YEARNED* FOR THE *HUMAN* WORLD AND *LEFT* ME.

HUH! WHAT THE HECK WOULD HE DO THAT FOR?

I DO NOT KNOW.

HE ONCE TOLD ME THAT HE SOUGHT IN *HUMAN* AFFECTION A WARMTH WHICH *MY* PEOPLE DON'T *POSSESS.*

I'VE NOT SEEN HIM IN MANY YEARS.

BUT HE'S STILL YOUR SON. YOU CAN *HELP* HIM.

NO. WHEN HE LEFT THE *UNDERWORLD,* HE *PUT* HIMSELF BEYOND MY *AID.*

I WILL NOT INTERFERE.

YEAH, I GET IT. AND YOU *REALLY* DON'T UNDERSTAND WHY HE LEFT?

I WILL DO *SOMETHING* FOR HIM.

I WILL LET *YOU* RETURN TO THE *WORLD ABOVE.*

I HAVE NO *ILLUSIONS* ABOUT HIS CHANCES WITH YOUR FELLOW *MORTALS...*

BUT PERHAPS YOUR COMPANY WILL MAKE HIS LAST DAYS *SWEETER.*

YEAH. THANKS A *BUNCH.*

OH, AND *MORTAL?*

YEAH?

IF HE HAS ANY *GLAMOUR,* IT IS A KIND NATURAL TO *YOUR* FOLK, NOT *MINE.*

"PERHAPS", THOUGHT COURTNEY, "IT WAS TRUE THAT HUMANS WERE MORE CAPABLE OF LOVE AND AFFECTION." THINGS THAT COURTNEY HAD KNOWN LITTLE OF UNTIL RECENTLY.

BUT THEY WERE CERTAINLY MORE CAPABLE OF CRUELTY AND VIOLENCE, AT LEAST, SO FAR AS SHE'D SEEN. EVEN THE WORST NIGHT THING SHE'D EVER MET WAS DRIVEN TO KILL BY SOME HUMAN MONSTER.

YOU *BLEW* IT, LEAVING *YOUR* PEOPLE TO BE WITH *US*.

WHAT'S *HERMIA HARKEN* EVER DONE FOR *YOU?*

SHE *LOVED* YOU, *DIDN'T* SHE?

COURTNEY UNDERSTOOD SKARROW'S SILENCE BETTER THAN ANY WORDS.

"THERE WAS SOMETHING ABOUT BEING CARED FOR," SHE THOUGHT. SOMETHING MAGICAL.

Creative writing: just because it happened to *you* doesn't make it interesting!

"SKARROW"...

BY...

UM ...COURTNEY CRUMRIN.

GO AHEAD, COURTNEY.

>SNORT<

HIS SWEETNESS SHINES LIKE A *LIGHT*...

FROM EYES OF BLACKEST...

...NIGHT.

AND WITHOUT A SINGLE *WORD*...

HE SAYS..

UM... HE SAYS... THE NICEST THINGS I'VE...

...EVER...

...HEARD.

>TITTER<

>SHHH<

DIMLY, AS COURTNEY READ AND THE HOTNESS OF EMBARRASSMENT FLUSHED HER FACE, SHE THOUGHT SHE COULD HEAR A THUNDERCLAP.

BUT PEOPLE FEAR AN OPEN HEART.

THE ROOM SEEMED TO DARKEN.

AND TEAR INNOCENCE APART.

HE'S CALLED A MONSTER BY THE FOOLS...

A DULL SENSE OF TOTAL HUMILIATION RESTED FIRMLY ON HER CHEST, MAKING BREATHING DIFFICULT, BUT SHE PLUNGED ON.

WHO TREAT HIS KIND LIKE PETS AND TOOLS.

ROLLING THUNDER SHOOK THE ROOM, AND THE CHAIRS BEGAN TO VIBRATE.

spak

COURTNEY BARELY NOTICED, HER ONE THOUGHT TO GET THROUGH HER STUPID POEM AND BE DONE WITH IT.

I WISH I KNEW THE PERFECT CHARM...

TO SAVE HIM FROM THOSE WHO MEAN HIM HARM.

Creati
because i
t mak
Courtney's Journal

MY GOODNESS. THAT WAS... POWERFUL STUFF, COURTNEY.

GOOD JOB.

PHEW.

WOW. THAT WAS A... REALLY COOL... ...POEM.

UH, THANKS.

DO YOU WANT TO WALK HOME WITH ME?

WHY?

WELL, CAUSE, LIKE, YOU'RE PRETTY COOL, AND... UM...

YOU KNOW THOSE GUYS THAT HANG OUT BY THE PLAYGROUND?

THEY'RE SCARED OF YOU, RIGHT?

YEAH, THEY ARE.

SO NOW, AFTER IGNORING ME ALL LAST YEAR, YOU'RE SUDDENLY MY BUDDY?

I GOT MORE IMPORTANT THINGS TO WORRY ABOUT THAN YOUR FIFTY-DOLLAR-A-DAY ALLOWANCE.

FINE! BE THAT WAY.

JERK.

POOR GIRL. WISH I COULD HELP.

I CANNOT TELL. I'VE BEEN BOUND TO SILENCE.

WASTE OF TIME.

PERHAPS YOU SHOULD LOOK TO SEE WHO HAD THE MOST TO GAIN FROM MY MISCHIEF.

WAIT A MINUTE!

YOU JUST *SAID* YOU'RE UNDER A *SILENCING* SPELL.

DON'T HELPFUL HINTS COUNT?

YES, WELL.

THAT SORT OF SPELL IS TRICKY. THERE'S ALWAYS A LOOPHOLE.

AHEM... UNLESS THE VICTIM DOESN'T WANT TO TALK.

...IF YOU FOLLOW ME.

HMM. I THINK I DO...

WHEN THE COVEN OF MYSTICS HELD COUNCIL, NOT ALL MEMBERS OF THE COVEN WERE EXPECTED TO APPEAR, BUT MOST DID THAT DAY.

MS. CRISP TOLD COURTNEY THAT THEY NEEDED REASSURANCE THAT THE COUNCIL WAS STILL IN AUTHORITY, AND THAT ALOYSIUS CRUMRIN WAS STILL ANSWERABLE TO THEM.

112

THE CURSE THAT HAS AFFLICTED ONE OF OUR NUMBER IS NO CREATION OF ANY SIMPLE CREATURE OF THE UNDERWORLD.

AND YET, SOME OF US STILL ARE BESET BY LIES, HANDED DOWN FROM OLDEN TIMES.

THE LIE PASSED DOWN THE GENERATIONS IS NO LESS UNTRUE THAN ANY OTHER SORT, THOUGH IT MAY BE HARDER TO DISCOVER. BUT IT IS OUR VERY PURPOSE TO DISPEL LIES, AND FIND THE TRUTH.

IT IS COMPLEX AND SUBTLE, DESIGNED FOR THE PURPOSE OF CONCEALING THE TRUTH AND PERPETUATING LIES.

DO NOT BE FOOLED, FOR IT'S VERY NATURE REVEALS IT.

JOHN MILTON MANDRAKE COUNCIL MEMBER 1278 - 2002

CHARLES LONDON COUNCIL MEMBER 1262 - 2002

THE NIGHT THINGS ARE NOT CREATURES OF DECEIT. THAT IS THE REALM OF MEN.

THE DARKNESS THAT WE SEEK TO KEEP AT BAY DOES NOT COME FROM THE UNDERWORLD. IT IS OUR DARKNESS, FROM WITHIN OUR OWN HEARTS.

THE SLAYING OF A SCAPEGOAT WILL NOT STOP IT. THAT PATH WILL ONLY FEED THE LIES.

MANDRAKE...

THANK YOU, PROFESSOR.

MARSHALL HUGHES, YOU MAY PROCEED WITH YOUR OPENING STATEMENT.

I THINK I'VE FIGURED IT OUT, THE CURSE.

YOU KNOW THOSE TWO COUNCIL GUYS THAT DIED?

WELL, WHO BENEFITS?

AND WHO'S BEEN HOVERING OVER HERMIA HARKEN SINCE SHE WAS FOUND?

IT'S WRATHUM, YOU KNOW, THE HEAD DUDE, 'CAUSE—

DON'T BE RIDICULOUS.

CONSIDERING HE APPOINTED BOTH THOSE COUNCIL MEMBERS, WOODRUE WRATHUM IS THE LEAST LIKELY SUSPECT.

HE'S PRAYING THE REST OF THE COUNCIL ACCEPTS HIS NEW APPOINTMENT. IF NOT, HE LOSES THE MAJORITY AND STOCKBROOK WILL BE VOTED COUNCIL HEAD.

BUT WHO WILL HE...?

THANK YOU, COUNCILMAN WRATHUM.

I'D LIKE TO BEGIN BY EXPRESSING MY UTMOST RESPECT FOR THE ESTEEMED PROFESSOR CRUMRIN. I DEEPLY REGRET THAT THESE MATTERS HAVE CAUSED HIM SO MUCH PERSONAL TURMOIL.

SUDDENLY, ALL BECAME SICKENINGLY CLEAR.

AND HECTOR'S GENTLE, TROUBLED EXPRESSION SEEMED SUDDENLY MASKLIKE, DISGUISING THE TWISTED SCHEMES BENEATH.

SURELY, HE WOULD BE COUNCILMAN WRATHUM'S NEW APPOINTMENT.

THE SESSION WENT ON FOR SEVERAL MORE HOURS.

ALOYSIUS PRESENTED HIS DETAILED KNOWLEDGE OF NIGHT THINGS, POINTED OUT THE LONG COMPANION-SHIP BETWEEN MADAM HARKEN AND SKARROW, WHICH HE'D SEEN FIRSTHAND. HE POINTED OUT HOW VAGUE THE EVIDENCE WAS FOR THE CREATURE'S GUILT, HOW THIN AND UNLIKELY ITS MOTIVATIONS.

HECTOR POINTED OUT HOW UNPLEASANT THE MATTER WAS, AND HOW RELIEVING IT WILL BE TO PUT IT BEHIND THEM ALL.

THE COUNCIL DELIBERATED FOR LESS THAN AN HOUR.

PROFESSOR, WE APPRECIATE YOUR EFFORTS, BUT I'M AFRAID WE FEEL YOU'VE LOST YOUR OBJECTIVITY IN THIS MATTER.

THE COUNCIL HAS AGREED UNANIMOUSLY THAT FOR THE SAFETY OF OUR COMMUNITY, YOU MUST RELINQUISH YOUR PRISONER TO US.

YES, COUNCILMAN.

THEY CAN'T—

COURTNEY, ALOYSIUS CAN'T STAND *ALONE* AGAINST THE WHOLE COVEN.

THEY'RE GOING TO *KILL* HIM! HE DIDN'T DO ANYTHING!

DON'T YOU *SEE*? THEY ALL *KNOW* THAT.

IT DOESN'T *MATTER* WHO CAST THE CURSE, WHAT *MATTERS* IS THAT THEY HAVE AN *EXCUSE* TO *PUNISH* YOUR FRIEND *SKARROW* FOR STEALING MADAM *HARKEN* AWAY, AND TO PUNISH *HERMIA* FOR CHOOSING A *NIGHT THING* OVER THE *COVEN*.

WHAT!?!

IT'S ONE THING FOR A MAN LIKE YOUR *UNCLE* TO WITHDRAW INTO SOLITUDE, BUT A WOMAN LIKE *HERMIA*— UNFORGIVABLE.

WHY?

FOR *STARTERS*, HERMIA BELONGED TO AN IMPORTANT *FAMILY*.

HER *FATHER* WAS THE HEAD OF THE *COUNCIL* BEFORE *WRATHUM*. HE'D PROMISED HER TO *MARRY*...

WELL IT'S *TOO LONG* A *STORY*.

SHE SIMPLY DIDN'T *WANT* THE LIFE *CHOSEN* FOR HER, SO SHE WALKED AWAY.

BUT *SKARROW!* WE CAN'T DO *ANYTHING?*

ALOYSIUS THOUGHT THEY'D *LISTEN* TO HIM.

HE *ASSUMED* THAT HE COULD SIMPLY *APPEAR* AND *EXPLAIN* IT ALL, AND THEY'D UNDERSTAND.

HE *MISCALCULATED.*

WELL I'M NOT GOING TO JUST *SIT* HERE.

COURTNEY!

TAKING THE ROAD, IT WAS A FIFTEEN-MINUTE WALK TO CRUMRIN HOUSE. COURTNEY MADE IT THERE IN FIVE.

YOU'VE GOT TO GO. *NOW!*

JUST RUN! GO HOME!

THEY WON'T FIND YOU THERE.

AS SKARROW CREPT SLOWLY AWAY TOWARD A DARK OPENING INTO THE EARTH, COURTNEY WONDERED HOW MUCH HE TRULY UNDERSTOOD OF HIS DANGER.

A FIGURE, JUST VISIBLE IN THE GLOOM, WAITED. COURTNEY COULD GUESS, OR HOPE, WHO IT MIGHT BE.

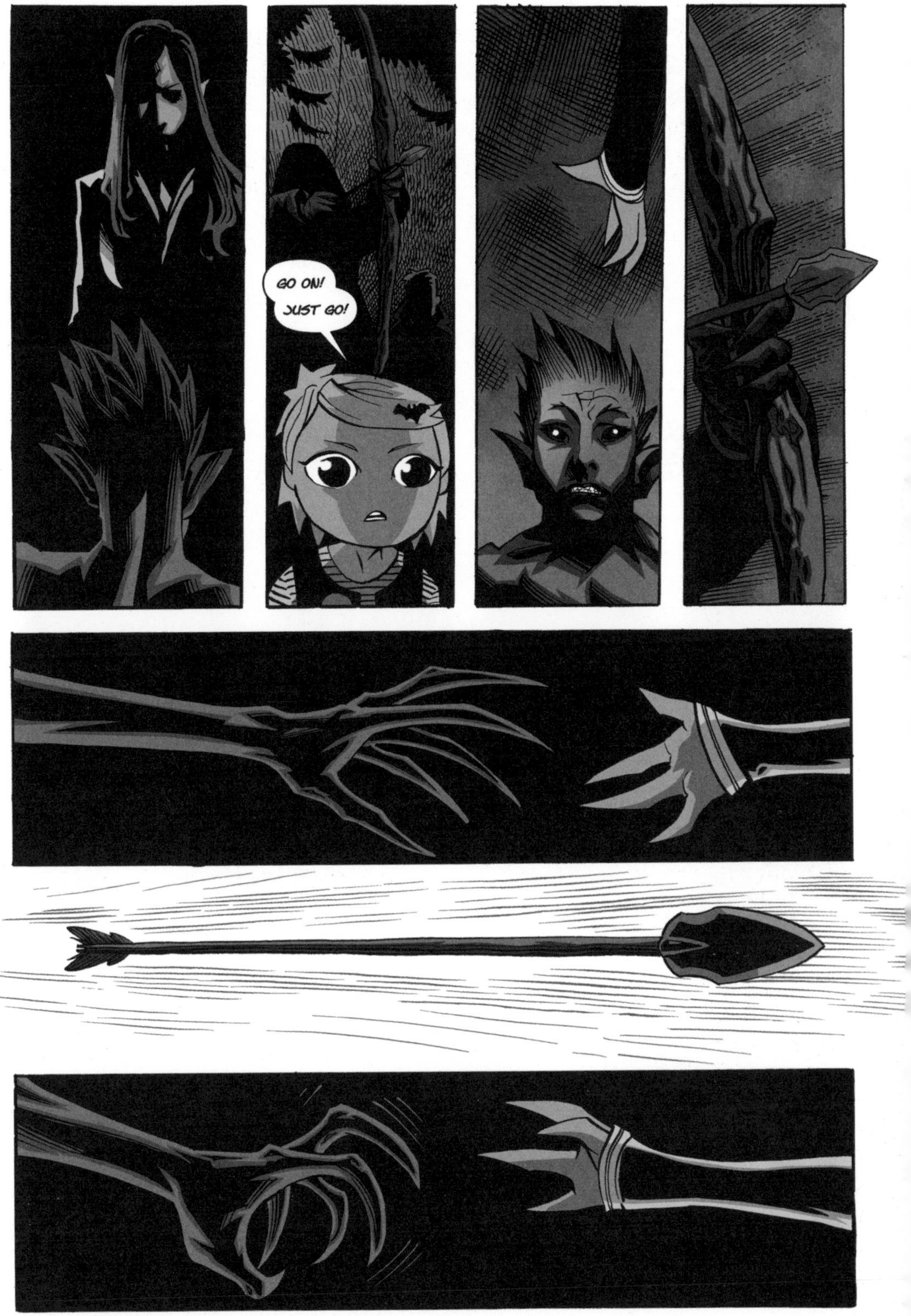
GO ON!
JUST GO!

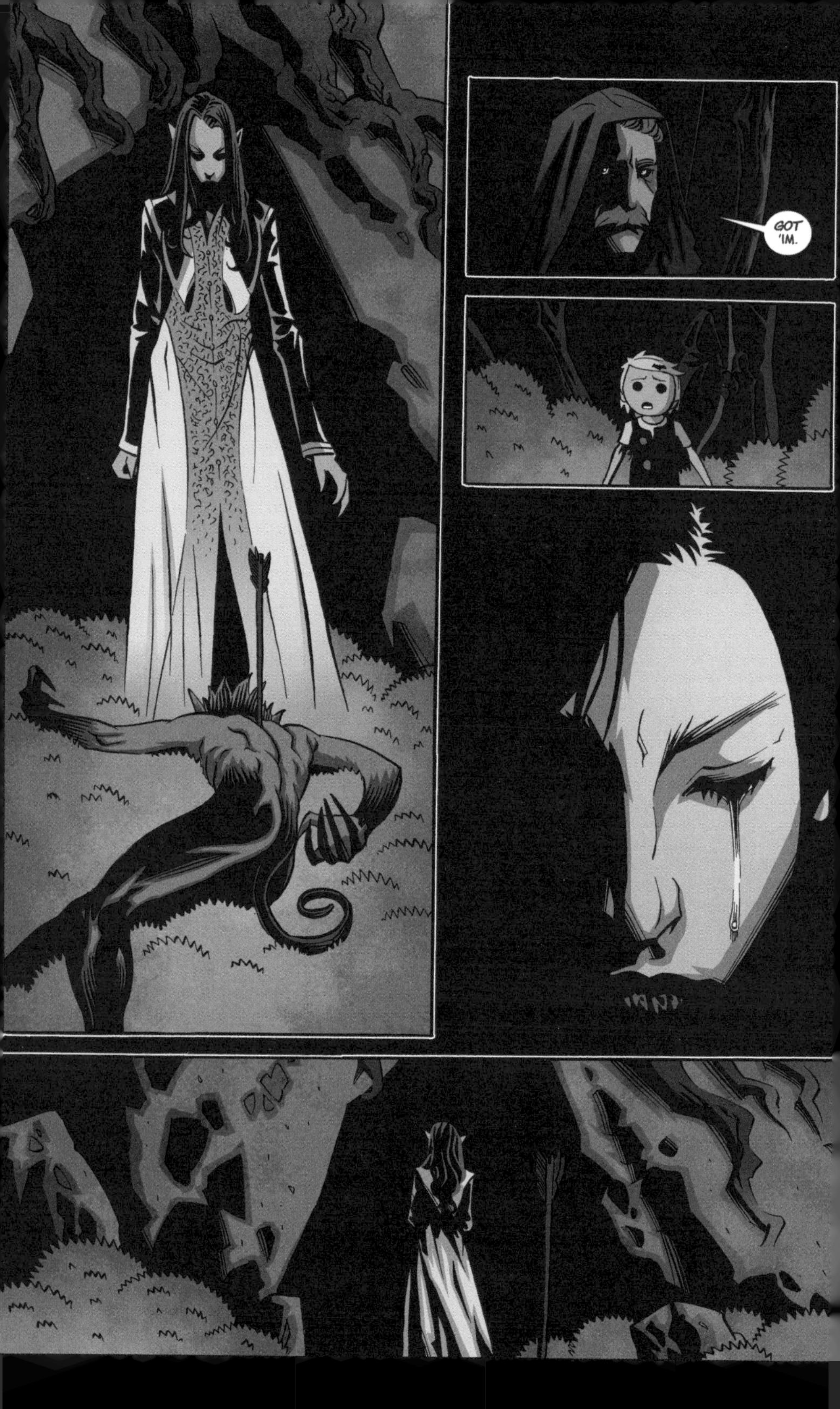
GOT 'IM.

A SAD WAY FOR THIS AFFAIR TO END.

WHY? YOU WANTED BLOOD, AND YOU GOT IT.

I HOPE TO HEAVEN YOU'RE SATISFIED.

THEY KILLED HIM!

THEY KILLED HIM!

THERE THERE, YOUNG LADY—

WOODRUE!! DON'T YOU DARE SPEAK TO MY NIECE!

I HATE YOU! I HATE YOU BOTH! HOW COULD YOU LET THIS HAPPEN!?!

I CAN ASSURE YOU—

WOODRUE.

GET OUT NOW, OR SO HELP ME....

A FEW DAYS LATER, IT WAS ANNOUNCED THAT THE CURSE WAS BROKEN.

THE FIRST THING MADAM HARKEN SAID WAS "YES," TO MARSHAL HECTOR HUGHES' PROPOSAL OF MARRIAGE.

COURTNEY LOOKED INTO HER EYES AND SAW A DEFEATED WOMAN.

LET'S GO BEFORE I PUKE.

IT'S NOT FAIR. SHE DIDN'T DO ANYTHING, SHE JUST DIDN'T WANT TO BE IN THEIR STUPID COVEN.

SHE TURNED HER BACK ON THE WORLD, JUST LIKE YOUR UNCLE. WHEN YOU DO THAT...

YOU CAN GET BITTEN ON THE ASS.

EXACTLY. WELL PUT.

COURTNEY WAS BEGINNING TO FIND MS. CRISP SOMEWHAT LESS AGGRAVATING LATELY, AND TALKING TO HER WAS ODDLY COMFORTING.

YOU SHOULD FORGIVE YOUR UNCLE, THOUGH.

HE LOVES YOU, AND THAT OUGHT TO COUNT FOR SOMETHING.

IT DOES.

BUT IT'S DEADLY TO TURN YOUR BACK ON A CRUMRIN.

HERMIA?

HERE I AM.

I MUST SAY, THIS IS ALL RATHER *MYSTERIOUS.* WHY THIS PLACE?

YOUR *NOTE* SAID TO MEET HERE. IS THIS YOUR ATTEMPT AT *ROMANCE,* HECTOR? IF *SO,* IT'S IN POOR TASTE.

MY NOTE?

BUT *I* WROTE NO NOTE.

I WROTE YOU *BOTH.*

WASN'T SURE IT'D *WORK*, BUT YOU *COVEN* PEOPLE ARE *NOTHING* IF NOT GULLIBLE.

YOUNG LADY, IF *THIS* IS YOUR IDEA OF A *JOKE*—

NO, YOU'RE THE JOKE!

ALL THIS PLANNING, ALL THE LIES AND MURDERS, JUST SO YOU COULD BE *TOP* OF THE *HEAP*.

CONGRATS. BET YOU HARDLY NOTICED IT WAS A HEAP OF *DOG CRAP*.

THAT'S NO WAY TO TALK TO—

SHUT UP!

I'M SICK OF YOUR BULL.

YOU FED IT TO *WOODRUE* AND THE *REST* OF 'EM, AND THEY WERE SO GRATEFUL THEY FOLLOWED YOU LIKE TRAINED MONKEYS.

BUT *NOT* RIGHT *NOW*. RIGHT *NOW* IT'S JUST YOU AND ME.

AND *WHAT* CAN *YOU* DO, *LITTLE GIRL*?

ME? NOT MUCH. I'M JUST A KID.

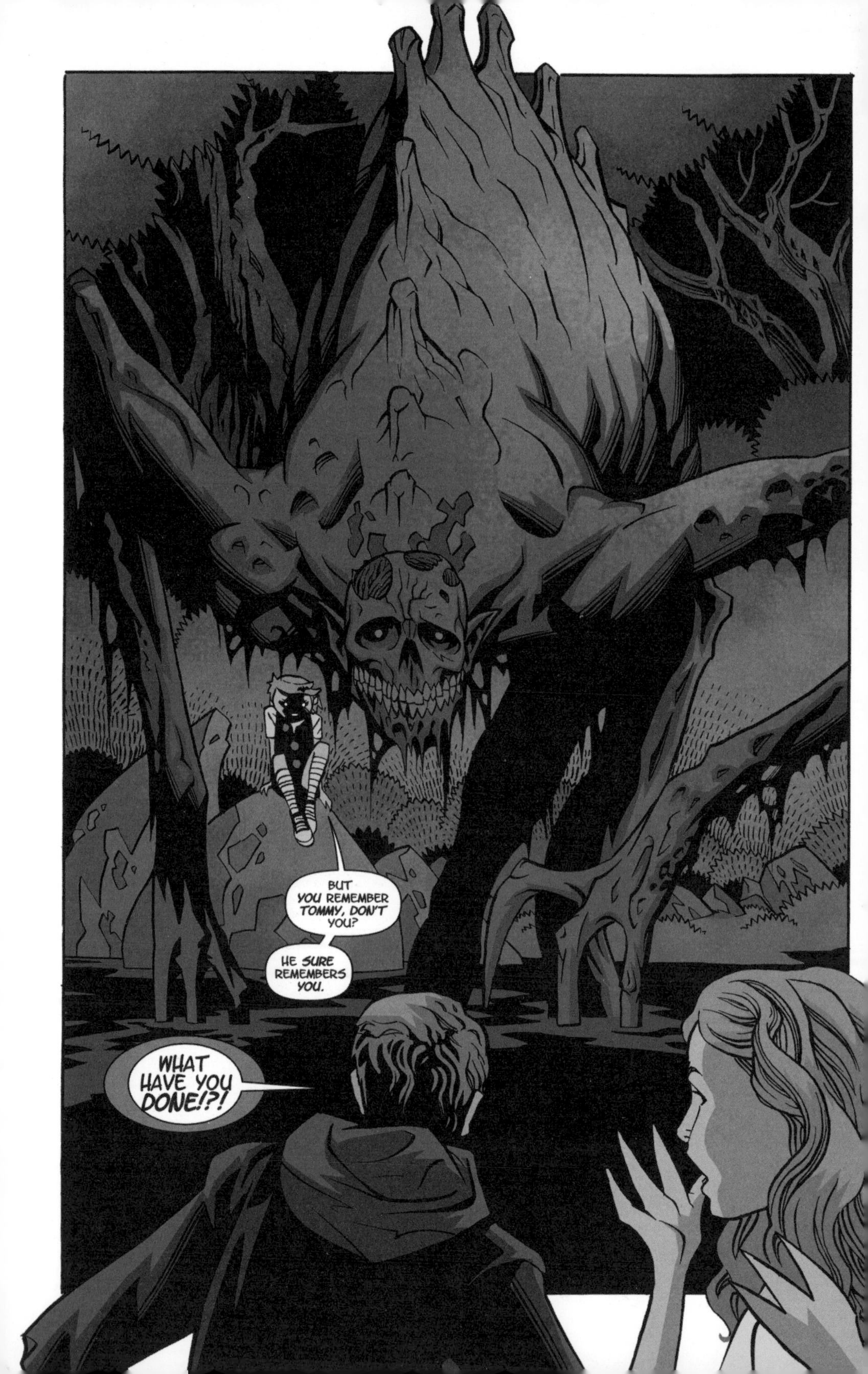
BUT YOU REMEMBER TOMMY, DON'T YOU?
HE SURE REMEMBERS YOU.
WHAT HAVE YOU DONE!?!

LADY...

GO AWAY AND *NEVER* COME BACK.

OR I'LL SEE THAT THEY BLAME *YOU* FOR THIS.

WHY? WHAT HAVE I DONE?

YOU'VE DONE *NOTHING.*

NOTHING TO SAVE SOMEONE WHO GAVE UP HIS *WORLD* TO BE WITH YOU.

HECTOR FORCED ME INTO IT.

WHAT *COULD* I HAVE DONE?

SOMETHING!

ANYTHING!!!

BUT YOU DID *NOTHING.* AND NOW YOU'VE *GOT* NOTHING.

WHAT'RE YOU GONNA DO ABOUT IT, SKINNY?

THAT'S CRUMRIN, REMEMBER?

OOOOH, I'M WETTING MYSELF.

WHAT'S SHE GONNA DO? GIVE US ALL NIGHTMARES?

YOU WANNA FIND OUT?

OH NO...

I'M SICK OF YOU GUYS.

I DON'T WANT TO HEAR ABOUT YOU BOTHERING PEOPLE ANYMORE.

IF I DO...

YOU'LL FIND OUT EXACTLY WHAT COURTNEY CRUMRIN CAN DO.

AND *THAT* WERE THE *WAY* OF IT.

NO ONE EVER *FOUND* WHAT BECOME OF OL' MARSHAL *HECTOR*.

AFTER 'IS *DISAPPEARANCE*, THEY FOUND SOME *MIGHTY* INCRIMINATIN' STUFF IN 'IS 'OME.

LOOKS LIKE PROFESSOR *CRUMRIN* WASN'T AS IRRATIONAL AS YOU *THOUGHT*, EH, WOODRUE?

POOR OL' *WOODRUE* DIDN'T COME OUT LOOKIN' TOO GOOD, *NEITHER*.

'COURSE THEY STILL HAD TO FILL THEM VACANT *SEATS* ON THE *COUNCIL*.

THEY *TRIED* ASKIN' OL' PROFESSOR *CRUMRIN*, FOR *SOME* SILLY REASON.

SLAMM!

BUT *EVENTUALLY* THEY MADE A MORE *PRACTICAL* CHOICE.

THANK YOU, GENTLEMEN.

I'LL GIVE YOUR OFFER *DUE* CONSIDERATION.

AND OF *COURSE*, NO ONE *EVER* SUSPECTED LITTLE MISS *CRUMRIN* O' FOUL PLAY.

WELL, ALMOST NO ONE.

Courtney Crumrin

By Ted Naifeh

The Coven of Mystics

Bonus Material & Cover Gallery

A pin-up drawing of Courtney Crumrin drawn in 2009.

Original Cover for *Courtney Crumrin and the Coven of Mystics*.

Cover for the French Edition of *Courtney Crumrin and the Coven of Mystics.*

Cover for Issue 1 of *Courtney Crumrin and the Coven of Mystics*.

Cover for Issue 2 of *Courtney Crumrin and the Coven of Mystics*.

Cover for Issue 3 of *Courtney Crumrin and the Coven of Mystics*.

Cover for Issue 4 of *Courtney Crumrin and the Coven of Mystics*.

TED NAIFEH

Ted Naifeh first appeared in the independent comics scene in 1999 as the artist for *Gloomcookie*, the goth romance comic he co-created with Serena Valentino for SLG Publishing. After a successful run, Ted decided to strike out on his own, writing and drawing *Courtney Crumrin and the Night Things*, a spooky children's fantasy series about a grumpy little girl and her adventures with her Warlock uncle.

Nominated for an Eisner Award for best limited series, *Courtney Crumrin*'s success paved the way for *Polly and the Pirates*, another children's book, this time about a prim and proper girl kidnapped by pirates convinced she was the daughter of their long-lost queen.

Over the next few years, Ted wrote four volumes of *Courtney Crumrin*, plus a spin-off book about her uncle. He also co-created *How Loathsome* with Tristan Crane, and illustrated two volumes of the videogame tie-in comic *Death Junior* with screenwriter Gary Whitta. More recently, he illustrated *The Good Neighbors*, a three volume graphic novel series written by *New York Times* bestselling author Holly Black, published by Scholastic.

In 2011, Ted wrote the sequel to *Polly and the Pirates*, and illustrated several *Batman* short stories for DC comics. In 2012, he wrapped up the *Courtney Crumrin* series in time for its tenth anniversary, and in 2014 he published two volumes of *Princess Ugg*. Currently, Ted is writing and illustrating two creator-owned series for older audiences: *Night's Dominion* and *Heroines*.

Ted lives in San Francisco, because he likes dreary weather.

Courtney Crumrin

VOLUME TWO

Crumrin

KEEP READING COURTNEY CRUMRIN:

MORE BY TED NAIFEH

For more information on these and other fine Oni Press comic books and graphic
novels, visit www.onipress.com. To find a comic specialty store in your area,
call 1-888-COMICBOOK or visit, www.comicshops.us.